THE
PIANO
TUNER

THE PIANO TUNER

A Novel

CHIANG-SHENG KUO

Translated by
Howard Goldblatt and Sylvia Li-chun Lin

Arcade Publishing • New York

First English-language Edition

This is a work of fiction. Names, places, characters, and incidents are either
the products of the author's imagination or are used fictitiously.

Arcade Publishing books may be purchased in bulk at special discounts
for sales promotion, corporate gifts, fund-raising, or educational purposes.
Special editions can also be created to specifications. For details, contact
the Special Sales Department, Arcade Publishing, 307 West 36th Street,
11th Floor, New York, NY 10018 or arcade@skyhorsepublishing.com.

Arcade Publishing® is a registered trademark of Skyhorse Publishing, Inc.®,
a Delaware corporation.

Visit our website at www.arcadepub.com.

10 9 8 7 6 5 4 3 2 1

Library of Congress Cataloging-in-Publication Data is available on file.
Library of Congress Control Number: 2022941812

Cover design by Erin Seaward-Hiatt
Cover illustration: Andy Ryan/Getty Images (woman); Eujarim
Photography/Getty Images (clouds)

ISBN: 978-1-956763-41-6
Ebook ISBN: 978-1-956763-60-7

Printed in the United States of America

THE
PIANO
TUNER

I

IN THE BEGINNING, we were souls without bodies. When God planned to give us souls a physical shape, we refused to enter into a concrete form that would fall ill and grow old, obstructing our free passage through time and space. God came up with a solution by having angels play enchanting music.

We souls were so spellbound by the music we wanted to hear it more clearly, which was possible only through one channel, the human ear. God's trick worked, and we souls gained a physical body.

What happened next ought to start with Rachmaninoff, heard through Lin *san*'s ears.

*

The music came from the second-floor practice room.

Lin had not heard the story of souls losing their freedom over a pair of ears. He had, in fact, just experienced a different kind of loss.

Three months after his wife's death, he'd finally pulled himself together enough to deal with the studio she'd run.

She had poured her heart and soul into the studio, attracting an enthusiastic following in the neighborhood. Then why hadn't she left a word about it during her last days? Maybe she'd felt bad about burdening him with the task of keeping the place going, he reflected. She knew that an amateur music lover like him would likely close up shop unless she asked him not to.

That speculation assuaged his guilt feelings somewhat, for, after all, before meeting Emily, he hadn't been able to tell a violin from a viola.

Three months had gone by and classes were ending. The instructors and students had all been notified of the closure.

It was the first time he'd been to the studio since her death, and he had waited until after nine at night, when the last session was over and he would not be subjected to reproachful looks from the newly jobless instructors. They would not say anything, but he would find their awkward attempts to avoid him unbearable.

His first marriage had lasted six years before ending in divorce. This one was over even sooner, a short four years, before Emily had time to turn him into a true lover of classical music. The cancer had come out of the blue and with a vengeance. She was gone in six months.

He was twenty years older than her. The thought of getting remarried had given him pause, fearing that one day he might be a burden to a young wife. He never imagined that it might end the way it did.

With the door to the practice room ajar, the lyrical notes of a piano came through crisply in the night air.

Emily had dragged him to a good many concerts, including her own recitals, but there were few pieces he could recognize right off. Surprised by the piano strains emerging from upstairs, he paused in his conversation with the studio manager and instinctively looked up in the direction of the music.

It was Rachmaninoff's "Song Without Words."

Emily's violin had introduced him to the tune on the eve of their first anniversary.

He'd gotten her a surprise gift, neither jewelry nor an expensive purse, but a self-sponsored recital. Overjoyed, she began by making him an audience of one in their living room, where she played the whole program for him. Only the Rachmaninoff piece inspired a strong reaction and deep emotions. The string version sounded unusually sorrowful, which may have led to thoughts of his mother, who had passed away a few years earlier.

"Seems awfully sad," he'd said.

Emily graciously replaced it with another selection for the recital. Yet the melody was etched on his mind. Like an audio allergen, an earworm, he seemed to hear it all the time; from a soprano's plaintive rendition to a cello performance, from car commercials to movie background music, the piece popped up around him in ever-shifting forms.

But on this night, when he heard the piano version in the empty studio, not only was it missing that grave quality, it actually sounded weightless, expansive, somewhat hazy.

"Who's that playing so late at night?" he asked the studio director.

From the moment he arrived, the moonfaced woman had tried to force a sad look onto her naturally happy countenance, but now, with this question taking her mind off her expression, she could relax.

"Oh, that's our piano tuner."

"Hasn't he been told to stop coming?"

"Yes, but he said he was happy to provide free service before the pianos are taken away."

Lin frowned but said nothing.

(God, what am I going to do with all the pianos?)

"He plays beautifully but said no when I asked if he'd like to offer lessons." She added, "Sometimes we let him use the room for free."

"How much do we pay him?"

"Fifteen hundred an hour."

Appallingly paltry pay compared to that of a teacher. A businessman at his core, Lin intuitively considered the difference in salary.

Having no piano of his own and refusing to teach, just happy to be a tuner. To Lin, that seemed irrational.

"He's pretty good."

He commented spontaneously. It was, after all, his music studio. If his judgment was off, so what?

"That's what Instructor Chen said too."

● Emily had always been Instructor Chen. He, on the other hand, had been the man behind the woman, old enough to be her father. So the staff called him Mr. Lin but called her Instructor Chen, as if unsure of their relationship.

He climbed the stairs slowly, drawn to the music.

It truly sounded different from the versions he'd heard, for there was a dreamy sweetness to it, like awakened memories of events long after they ended.

(Sooner or later these melodies too will disappear from my life.)

When he reached the top of the stairs, he looked into the only lighted practice room. A man in a baseball cap sat at the upright piano just beyond the partly opened door.

Lin recognized the piano, a Bösendorfer.

After a while, Emily, a student of the violin, had rarely sat at a piano. In the end, the Steinway at their house had been used only by her accompanist during practice.

She'd studied both the piano and violin as a child and had double-majored in high school. Lin once asked her why she'd settled on the violin, to which she'd given a half-serious answer: she could never hope to be a concert pianist, but maybe she could audition her way into an orchestra and make a living with a violin.

He let it go at that, assuming she'd probably considered not returning when she was studying abroad. She might have had a Caucasian boyfriend at the time. At thirty-six, Emily should have known that her prospects would continue to diminish if she did not get married.

He'd bought the new Steinway grand after they were married. The secondhand Bösendorfer she'd been playing up to that time was moved to the studio. Back then, visiting friends had been impressed by how he doted on his wife.

There was another reason for his extravagance. A self-made businessman, he had built an export empire selling plastic lounge chairs during the economic boom of the 1980s. Made in Taiwan. That was how small and medium-sized businessmen of his generation made their fortunes. They traded in household implements and electronics, but none could make automobiles or, for that matter, pianos for export.

A piano does not age, not with meticulous care and tuning, and will always produce notes as perfect as the day it was made, even better if played by a pair of powerful, agile, magical hands.

He had to laugh as he listened to notes flow from the Bösendorfer's keys, each as bright and clear as polished glass.

The ideal climate for the Steinway at home was twenty degrees Celsius with 42 percent humidity. But over the past six months, he'd been negligent in caring for the instrument.

The old piano, in de facto exile, had been diligently maintained here while a layer of dust covered the Steinway, its keys out of tune, its strings out of shape. He mulled the irony in his aching heart until he tasted a rust-tinged sourness.

(I'm all alone again, a sixty-year-old man.)

He was reminded of the old Yamaha at home when he was a child.

His sister had been given piano lessons. In his father's circle of old-fashioned doctors, playing the piano was preparatory work for a daughter's future marriage. With a piano in her dowry, she would be recognized as well brought up. His parents never realized how poorly cut out she was for the piano. She'd failed the high school entrance exam three times before they sent her to Japan. He could recall seeing his sister, a butterfly bow in her hair, sitting at the piano practicing a Schubert piece over and over. Why hadn't his parents sent him with her for piano lessons? They favored boys over girls and had expected him to get into Jianguo High School and then the Engineering Department at Taiwan University. He had not let them down.

He wondered if, at some level, he'd married Emily to make up for missing out on music. Though fully aware that the Bösendorfer was quite serviceable, he nonetheless believed that a musician ought to have a grand, not an upright, at home. When he thought back now, he had to concede that it might not have been entirely for her sake, that it had also been the result of a sense of vanity of which he himself was only dimly aware.

Rachmaninoff had led him into a momentary confusion of memories.

As the final notes lingered, the pianist's hands gently took flight, like riding on invisible clouds, made an arc in the air, and landed on his knees.

Lin stood outside the door, quietly watching the man's ending gesture.

That must have been when he became aware of my existence.

In the days to come, in the small pub we frequented, he once shared his view that some musical instruments are perfect matches for the female body, like the flute or a harp.

Lin *san* enjoyed seeing a slender, graceful woman play the violin, as opposed to a hulking man, who, with his head tilted to one side, could crush the instrument on his shoulder. He considered it inelegant for a woman to play the cello, her legs spread around the instrument.

Privately, he thought a piano's form fit men better, especially a grand, which only large hands, long arms, and broad shoulders can fully control.

I jerked my head around when I sensed someone at the door.

"Oh, sorry—"

I'd been coming to the studio for over a year and had run into him a few times when he dropped Emily off. But this was the first time we'd actually met.

The face behind the steering wheel, coupled with his silvery gray hair, had always looked off-putting and cold. I was surprised to see that, out of his Ferrari, he was actually half a head taller than me. Face-to-face with a man who had just lost his wife, I took pains to not seem gratuitously sympathetic.

"I want to thank you. The director told me you're the one who's been taking care of these pianos."

"I took on some of the former tuner's clients when he retired."

We fell silent, until I turned at the door, canvas bag over my shoulder,

"How's the Steinway at home, Mr. Lin?"

2

THE GREEK MATHEMATICIAN Pythagoras was said to have walked by a blacksmith shop one day in 530 BCE, and was mesmerized by the forging sound, ugly and jarring at times and yet, to his surprise, elegantly harmonious at others. When he walked in for a closer look, he discovered that the weight of the hammer was the key, producing different sounds depending upon the force used by the blacksmith.

Lovely sounds emerged if the ratio of two hammers' weights happened to be 2:1, 3:2, or 4:3, thus forming the basics for tuning a keyboard instrument.

Two harmonious notes produce the resonance of a perfect strike ratio.

What was it that ultimately moved the souls when they received the ears they coveted?

Was it similar only to the molecular vibrations from a pebble tossed into a placid lake? Or was it a frequency that has always existed in the universe, something one can experience even without a physical body?

Each piano string is under 160 pounds of pressure, which comes to approximately twenty tons of pressure for all 230 strings.

While creating a melodious timbre, the instrument itself must withstand immensely painful tension. The difference between a tuner and a pianist may very well lie in how they perceive the mechanics involved.

An expert tuner spurns a tuning fork and relies only on his ear, itself a rare talent. Using equal temperament, a tuning fork distributes the twelve semitones equally in an octave, so each note turns out to be a semitone that is one twelfth lower.

Therefore, not a single piano in the world has perfect pitch, and a pianist can produce only notes modified by a tuner.

Without a piano of my own, I play when I tune, and that has been pretty much how I've been able to practice over the years.

More than once, bewildered clients have been about to say something when they hear, to their surprise, the unexpected quality of music I produce on their instruments.

I could guess what they were thinking: how could he be content to be a mere piano tuner? Some have eagerly asked if I'd studied with a famous pianist.

What they do not understand is how difficult it is to be an expert tuner. A great many famed pianists employ the same tuner, for a top tuner is harder to come by than a first-rate pianist. A fact the world has overlooked.

More people want to give a concert than the proverbial carps in a river, and, with enough nerve, anyone can play on a stage. A tuner not only has to be a piano expert but must be familiar with all the pieces a pianist performs at each concert. Needless to say, he must know by heart their individual styles as well as their interpretation of each piece of music.

Continuous practice is crucial if one wants to be a tuner like that.

Naturally, being in a class of one's own remains a dream.

I chose to give up the better-paid job of piano teacher and become a tuner, a worker not an artist, in people's eyes, simply because I had a hard time dealing with the parents. I could not bring myself to praise or encourage their talentless children just so I could continue to earn a fee.

What concerned me more was the damage to my keen ear by their playing, more like banging, actually. I could even suffer irreparable mental and bodily injury.

*

In theory, as the owner of a Steinway, Emily could have a technician from the company provide reliable tuning service and repair, but she was dissatisfied with the instrument's tonal quality.

I heaved a heartfelt sigh when I opened the lid to study the hammers the first time I'd touched the Steinway after its owner fell ill.

"Too humid."

The company technicians had not known what Emily wanted, failing to understand what she meant by the action being too noisy, by the high notes being too thin or the low notes lacking the full-bodied resonance she sought. It was beyond them to know the causes of these issues or to comprehend the buttery notes she was after.

In the end, their only response would be, Our brand is the finest in the world. Or, Didn't you notice these issues when you bought it?

In the end, Emily decided to give the newbie, the tuner at her music studio, a shot at her Steinway.

"Did you find the problem for her?"

Lin *san* watched and listened as I opened my tool kit, a dubious look on his face, as if straining to imagine how Emily had suffered feelings of helplessness, was crestfallen, even angry, because of the piano.

"It's probably more appropriate to say adjusting the tune than tuning."

I went on to explain why it wasn't enough for the

technician to tune only by equal temperament or just intonations. Sometimes it is important to also hear the overtones, since we play chords on a piano. A few notes, because of the frequency of vibration in individual pitches, will eventually be in conflict.

Lin *san* tried to focus on what I was saying, but the technical terms were too complex for him to grasp. Besides, he hadn't been sleeping well for weeks. He looked more haggard than when I'd run into him at the studio that time.

He knew his wife was the tense, anxious type, even though she'd always presented a charming, graceful smile to the outside world. Yet he'd never heard her complain about the piano, a detail hidden from him until this day.

What was buried deep in daily life had yet to be unveiled when the marriage ended. He could not have imagined how flawed that Steinway was to her, how utterly lacking in the tones she'd wanted.

"But Emi—my wife, she, why didn't she know all this?"

I saw him secretly stifle a yawn.

"Most people who play an instrument know little about it.

"The perfection a musician pursues is both abstract and idiosyncratic, which in the end is realized in a mechanical installation created purely based on physics. It is a fact that musicians often overlook," I said.

He did not ask any more questions.

Maybe my answer gave him the impression that a

piano wasn't our real topic, only a hint that related to the rest of his life.

Seeing his downcast, wretched look, I could almost hear him mutter to himself, How could I let a total stranger see the ignorance that kept popping up in my life? How is that possible?

He was seeing other women when he first went out with Emily.

One of them was the owner of a Japanese izakaya on Anhe Road. They had known each other for more than a decade since the night he happened to walk in shortly after his divorce. When they were feeling down or lonely, they served one another as a convenient "fire extinguisher." Another was a PR consultant at a major banking group. He was quite aware that she may have had an ulterior motive in being with him.

Then there was the interior designer, a woman who had gained a bit of fame.

After his mother's death, his impulsive nature led to the abrupt decision to move back to his childhood home, an old, single-story house, part of which had held his father's clinic. He hired the interior designer, Beatrice Huang—don't ask me why these women all have English names—to renovate the house from top to bottom. The end result, a stylish house replete with postmodern nostalgia, even made the cover of an architectural magazine. He hosted a party for Beatrice in his newly remodeled house. Maybe it was his way of showing that love was not essential, but what really counted was his initial declaration that he would never remarry. He may not have admitted it to himself, but it was possible that he married Emily barely six months after they'd met largely because he did not know how to end his relationship with Beatrice.

Musicians don't always know their pianos. They often project too much of their emotions onto it, forgetting that it's just a machine controlled by a series of hammers, devoid of arcane principles.

In that vein, a common mistake by ordinary people is failing to see how complex and unpredictable the human heart is; they seem to believe in the existence of music scores that will teach them how to deal with one another.

What Lin *san* never quite grasped was, every time he got involved with a woman, a group of strangers would force their way into his life, and he would be dragged into their social circle. He was surrounded by designers and architects when he was dating Beatrice. After marrying Emily, he learned that musicians are not the hermitic type; in fact, they have seemingly endless social engagements, constant recitals, and premiere receptions.

He actually had few friends of his own.

In light of the economic tsunami that hit shortly after his remarriage, he decided to shutter his thirty-year-old company. He'd thought he would live the life of an urbane retiree and be the driving force behind a successful violinist. In the end, however, he was mired in loneliness he did not understand.

He had been entertaining clients at a Michelin-class French restaurant the night he met Emily. After the meal came a wine-tasting the owner had arranged. In addition to a limited-edition cellared whisky that had been flown in from Scotland, he had also invited a string quartet for background music.

Emily, the only female musician, was wearing a full-length, demurely sleeveless black dress. With her long hair braided and pinned back in the princess style, she affected a look of elegance. One of his clients exclaimed,

"What a pretty girl. Why not ask her to join us?"

That troubled Lin *san*, who found the man's attitude odious. What did he think she was? Though he'd been a businessman for decades, he'd never completely freed himself from the constraints of his doctor father's strict upbringing. Granted, he'd been imperceptibly influenced by his father's brand of male chauvinism, but he was contemptuous of men who harassed women or frequented brothels.

He may have owed his self-assurance to his appearance: Over six feet tall, he had thick brows and a high nose bridge. Nature had been kind to let him keep his full head of silvery, wavy hair even late into his fifties. He drew looks wherever he went.

Glancing at Emily, who was engrossed in her music, playing with her eyes closed, he was momentarily reminded of his young sister in Japan, whom he hadn't seen for a long time. His father might well have hoped for his sister to be like the woman in front of him. The client was too important to offend, and Lin *san* struggled internally before quietly bringing up the shameful request with the restaurant manager. "Just that, nothing more. We think she's very talented . . ." He was digging himself into a deeper and deeper hole as he went on.

Likely a common occurrence in such a place. The manager smiled and eased him out of his distress. "Inviting only her would not look good, Chairman Lin. Why don't I set up a table next to yours and invite all four of them? I can bring you a bottle of Chivas Regal or perhaps . . . ?"

Moments later, Emily and her fellow musicians came up to offer a toast. Her eyes met his, and she seemed to know instinctively that he was not someone who would be difficult. Ignoring his clients, he let his chauvinist side take over as he dragged a chair up for her to sit near him.

We can agree that frequency vibrations do indeed occur between two souls. Emily's well-trained ears as a musician must have heard them.

Unable to hear what she was playing, she could not know what was wrong with the piano's pitch.

She thought she'd finally realize her dream of becoming

a performing musician, with Lin *san* as her sanctuary. At a very young age she had been in classes for musical prodigies and had later earned a music MFA overseas. Yet all she could get were part-time instructorships in college music departments and invitations to join colleagues' string quartets.

Lin *san* would have heard what I heard if he'd been favored with more advanced musical appreciation.

There was an internal dissonance, out of tune with her soul's frequency.

When I was done I put my tools away.

An autumnal afternoon sun slanted in through the French doors. Beyond them stood an old, energetic-looking plane tree. Few people could afford a house with such a large yard in the downtown area. I was sweating a bit, either because of my intense focus on the job or from the heat of the sun's rays. I removed my cap to cool off.

"Oh, I thought—"

He looked too embarrassed to finish.

"What's that?"

He said the cap had him mistaking me for a twenty-something.

No, I'm in my forties, I said.

My balding head does not lie. Not everyone is lucky enough to have a full head of silvery hair in his late fifties. Mine had begun to fall out, in handfuls, when I turned thirty. I tried to envision how I must have looked in his eyes. Besides my baldness, I was graced by a pair of jug ears and a pitted face from the assault of acne in puberty.

I knew that, if not for my homely appearance, his male instinct would have caused him to be suspicious of me when he learned, for the first time, of the many trips his wife's piano tuner had made to his house.

He took out his wallet, but I said no. It's free. I was grateful for Instructor Chen's trust in me, and this is the least I could do to repay her.

3

I THINK MOST READERS will be more interested in someone like Lin *san* than in me when they reach this point of the story. Am I right?

I have enough self-awareness to know that I'm not the protagonist. Without at least a speck of such wisdom, my life would likely be worth less than it is now.

That said, as the narrator, I do see that what I'm doing now isn't all that different from the job of a piano tuner.

With a piece of music that has touched the souls over the centuries, everyone remembers the composer's extraordinary talent and the performer's outstanding skill. No one ever thinks of the role played by a tuner. As a matter of fact, knowing their status, the tuners themselves are used to remaining behind the scene.

A successful performance requires precise temperament

and harmonious timbre. Likewise, a captivating story needs a narrator who knows moderation, who is able to trim off unrelated, trivial details, and who can find the right focus and pace but refrains from embellishment or willful attempts to give the tale a self-proclaimed happy ending.

I've been accustomed to staying hidden from sight all these years, but I know that everything has its own basic, professional demands. If a musician is unhappy with a particular performance, the tuner must share the blame. If a story fails to please or earn the reader's trust, the narrator is to be held partly responsible.

Hence, a responsible narrator probably should not shun the first-person narrative perspective or reject all questions or criticism. Therefore, I think it's only right that I tell you a bit about myself.

I was, in fact, a music prodigy.

I've tried hard to keep it a secret, but now it has to come out.

It's a secret not because I never wanted anyone to know. The truth is, after a while, no one cared or mentioned it, so it evolved into a fragment from the past that only I remember but don't feel like talking about.

There was a time when my talent was not a secret, for word of it circulated widely in my elementary school. It's been so long now that everyone has forgotten about it.

Once, in second grade, I walked up to the piano and played the song the music teacher had just taught us to sing, while all the other kids ran off as soon as the session was over.

The teacher, who walked in to prepare for her next class, was stunned by the music that flowed from the little boy's hands, not just single notes, but chords.

Soon they discovered that I had rare, ultrasensitive ears, and that my ability to remember notes far exceeded that of other kids of my age.

And there was more. I had powerful hands that were wider, with longer fingers, than other children. I was born with all the requirements to be a musical prodigy, all except for family.

My parents snorted at the teacher who came to see them. What could I get out of playing the piano? Could I run faster than bullets when war broke out?

Father lost the sight in one eye during the Second Taiwan Strait Crisis of August 23, 1958. When he was discharged, he brought his local Kinmen bride to Taipei and settled down in a shantytown that was later razed. He opened a dumpling shop to support a family of seven. In his view, the three boys should all attend military academies, while he let fate decide for the girls, who would go to a public, tuition-free teachers' college if their scores were good, or get married at seventeen if not.

My musical talent did not bring him a shred of pride. On the contrary, it was more like a ticking time bomb, a threat that one day his prodigal son would abandon him, and that gave birth to latent violence and real tension between us that could erupt at the slightest provocation.

I did not take music lessons in school.

Along the way, there were always kind teachers who saw my situation and offered free lessons. Even now I can imagine the white and black piano keys and, recalling the notes in my head, play any music I want on a desktop. For me that's easy.

During my indifferent childhood, I did not think much about my inexplicable talent, since for me it was like riding a bike or whistling. In the beginning, I even believed every kid could learn to do it.

At home, Father did not know how to deal with his oddball son, so he flew into a rage whenever he saw me hanging out at the dumpling shop, fingers thrashing in the air as if racked by epileptic spasms.

At school, I stood out because my teacher offered me free piano lessons when she had the time. Did that mean the other kids had to pay for theirs? I was so dense.

They were taken by their parents to study with this or that teacher in the hope that they would pass an entrance exam to the highly competitive music program in middle school. It, too, was a mystery to me at first, for I thought playing the piano was for nothing but my own private enjoyment. It was wondrous and joyful to be one with the music, so why must it become a battle over grades?

I grew increasingly taciturn.

Shortly before I graduated from elementary school, the music teacher took me to a piano recital. In his early twenties, the pianist, the first-place winner in an International Chopin Competition, was a young man with the same skin tone and hair color as me.

He'd been born in Hanoi, Vietnam, also into an impoverished family, my teacher told me. Later, he'd met a renowned music teacher who had helped get him into the Moscow Tchaikovsky Conservatory, from which he had emerged a few years later with budding renown of his own.

It was a fantastic story, but it failed to make me envious or aspirational. Hanoi or Moscow, both were too abstract, too unreal for me. What I never forgot were the sparkles that seemed to shoot from his fingertips. It was my first concert, and the performance brought me to tears.

After the recital, my teacher, Ms. Chiu, treated me to an ice cream sundae at Fule on Dunhua North Road. It was an unforgettable afternoon. Her long hair shone softly under the sun, reminding me of the glossy black piano on the stage.

I ate with gusto, smearing the corners of my mouth with whipped cream, which she then wiped off with a handkerchief. I heard her mutter something I remember even now.

"Ai, just a little boy."

I could play Beethoven's "Moonlight Sonata" by then.

After the ice cream treat, we strolled down the wide sidewalk on Dunhua Road. I ran off after a dragonfly, but she called me back.

"Promise me to never give up the piano, will you? Hook our pinkies?" she said.

I had no idea what a weighty promise I'd made that day. Her endearing sigh, when I think about it now, years later, decided the next step in my life.

She paid her college teacher out of her own pocket to take me on as a pupil. Obviously, she could not have imagined the kind of life I would have in the section for students considered unteachable, given my below-average performance in every subject but music.

I became the unlucky target of class bullies who had too much energy. The bell that rang after each class made me fret over where to hide for the next ten minutes. Skinny as a bamboo pole, I was also badly disfigured by acne during those years. One of my worst fears was that they'd find out I was pompous enough to play the sissy piano after school.

At fourteen, I was already exhausted from evading their harassment. Added to that were the never-ending sounds of chopping pork in the kitchen, the clamor from diners placing their orders and getting their checks, pranks played by classmates with raging hormones, and loud engines and honking motor vehicles out on the street. I was so drained I just wanted a quiet place where I could put on my headphones and push the unbearable boredom away, further and further away, as far as possible.

The dashing professor often charged his students additional fees to hold flashy recitals at his house on Yangmingshan. Those who ponied up a fee took center stage and played a few solo pieces for the audience.

Why did the parents look more tense than their performing children? It took me a while to figure out that the professor had been hinting that they must start making connections for their children, and that these recitals were a vital investment, for he invited important figures to offer "valuable advice."

I did not know who those "important figures" were, but I can still recall how they praised all the students to high heaven, claiming that every one of them would be the next classical music superstar. As the only one who was out of step, sometimes I let slip a yawn over an insipid performance or sniggered when I overheard the excessive praise.

My inability to pay the fees and my terrible attitude turned me into an object of scorn among the students. I couldn't even tell Ms. Chiu about all the ridiculous things I discovered.

Had she gone through a similar initiation rite? If I were to reveal my contempt for these people, would I be mocking and hurting her feelings? I wondered if she too had dreamed of international fame or of participating in a Chopin competition.

I, however, was relieved at the same time.

It was clear to me that I did not belong there.

4

L ET's go into a robust, abundant forest and pick out a
tree for a lumberjack to cut down and send to a mill.

A designer begins work on a resonating chamber and
soundboard before a carpenter and blacksmith take over.
Wire after wire, screw after screw, the hammer system is
formed and swirls are carved into the instrument. Then a
tuner arrives to set the tones.

And there you have it, a piano.

Some may not agree that a piano is a mere mechanical
object; to these people, a piano is infused with a unique
spirituality by each participant in the complex, delicate
construction process, from the lumberjack to the mover at
the end. They know it's not an automobile or a television
set, for neither has such a mysterious and sacred aura.

Yet, even the aura cannot alter the fact that every piano

31

has its own timbre, a fact unknown to many people, who continue to believe that every note they hear is accurate and perfect. And that is the power of civilization.

To be frank, humanity is another object with innate imperfections. We, too, decorate it with abstract terms like soul, sacred, love, and beauty, don't we?

Isn't civilization forever training us to treat many things with deep-seated respect and awe, and leave no room for doubt?

The old tuner who taught me everything I know about the profession once told me that the relationship between a piano, a musician, and a tuner is very much like that between a marriage counselor and a couple.

When a neurotic pianist is fixed up with an imperfect piano, the major task of a piano tuner is to help them sketch out the happy contours of what they can attain together.

The key is, the tuner himself does not have to be perfect; it is sufficient for him to have a pair of ears that can detect the vibrations from two flawed objects.

If you asked me why I worked so hard at becoming a piano tuner instead of striving for the higher calling of a pianist, that would probably be my answer.

Lin slept soundly the night after he hired someone to service the Steinway. He woke up the next morning, somewhat relieved of the weariness that had set in over the past few days.

As he drank his coffee, he gazed at the piano in the living room as a dream from the night before slowly came back to him. In it, Emily, in the black full-length dress she'd worn the night they'd met, stood beside the piano playing her violin. The scene was soundless, her facial expression blurred. The more he tried to see clearly, the hazier it got.

As his gaze drifted, he saw that Emily's accompanist was not the woman she had played with for years. It was a stranger, whose figure and appearance kept changing until Emily held up her bow and, with a smile, made the introduction. He looked again at the person at the piano, who turned out to be the man in a baseball cap.

To Lin, it could have been a sign that maybe he shouldn't close up shop just yet.

He recalled their conversation before the tuner left the studio.

"If you're planning to sell the Bösendorfer, would you let me know?" he'd asked.

"Are you interested in buying it?"

"No, that's beyond me. I'm just hoping, um, well, if I know where it's going, maybe I can continue to tune it."

(He has formed a bond with the piano!)

Lin thought he understood how the younger man felt.

He was a businessman, after all, and he had a few ideas

about what to do with the music studio; he just couldn't make up his mind which one he should choose.

Best if someone took it over, but he'd never forgive himself if a new sign were hung above all of Emily's hard work. There was a year left on the lease, and if he shuttered the studio, he could not think of another business that would find the space suitable.

The tuner's wish had alerted him to something.

If the space had to be emptied, he wouldn't mind selling the Yamahas, but the Bösendorfer was a different matter, for it had accompanied Emily in her life in music.

She had owned the Steinway at home for less than five years, while the old Bösendorfer had been with her for nearly three decades. But how was he going to care for two pianos? The old family house he'd inherited from his parents couldn't possibly accommodate another addition.

He was once again disconsolate as he reconsidered his plans.

(So, am I to just keep going like this, alone?)

Surveying the room, he tried to envision how it would look with two pianos crammed into that space. What kind of life would he have, hemmed in by two huge instruments?

Now that all the classes had been terminated, the director and bookkeeper came for an inventory and to square accounts. The studio was quiet and empty after dark.

He had gotten into the habit of sitting in the studio at night, usually at the Bösendorfer.

Ever since learning about his wife's borderline neurotic demands for the Steinway, he had begun to feel different about it.

(Why had she never mentioned it?)

He painstakingly scrolled through his memory to conjure up how Emily had looked sitting at a piano but managed only to uncover fragmented images of her shortly after their marriage, when she was still teaching, playing along with her students. He wondered how those students had fared. They probably did not know that their teacher had died.

Emily had not wanted to take on any more students after the Bösendorfer was replaced by the Steinway. That had come as a surprise, but he'd supported her decision, of course, and encouraged her to focus on her own performance.

His ever-eager preparation for the solo recital had followed. Since professional music reviews had not yet begun appearing in media outlets, her recital had drawn little attention. Forty percent of the tickets had been given away, while another 40 percent were taken by business associates. Who had actually bought tickets?

Strangers who had just happened upon the posters? Or old friends who had been quietly following her life from a distance?

Had they stopped seeing each other, would he still have bought a ticket and quietly sat in the audience after just happening to learn about the recital?

*

He'd been to more concerts with her than he could count, from international masters to no-name students. For the latter, the room would be filled with friends and family. Murmured old-womanish gossip came from all directions—someone's son was heading to Europe, someone else's daughter was marrying so-and-so's son—but not a word about that day's performance, as if this were the only way to lessen the awkwardness of obligatory attendance.

If it had been a concert by a famous musician, he would be treated to a different spectacle, one unique to Taipei. There would be a large turnout of high officials, as if being there proved that they were in step with the world and could boast a connection to the master musician. Anybody who was anybody would not want to miss such an event, turning it into a novel kind of family gathering.

Aware of his status as a businessman, and not outgoing by nature, he always sat quietly, while Emily was on hand to mingle with the important people.

He wasn't ignorant of the fact that he'd known very little about her life before their marriage.

That did not bother him, since he was twenty years older than her. He'd seen enough in his line of work that he did not need to know everything to feel reassured. Fight when you can and retreat when you must was his philosophy. For someone with his background, taking music lessons largely guaranteed a particular kind of upbringing.

Emily, who had received an MFA in America, was obviously less complex than the women he'd met in his old social circle.

Every woman in his life had wanted something from him.

That included Emily. She would not otherwise have been interested in dining with a man two decades her senior, would she? Then again, without supply and demand, there would be no genuine connections between people, would there?

Beatrice Huang had wanted nothing but a man who existed only in her romantic fantasies. His first wife had been an outstanding student in the Foreign Languages Department at his university. Over the years, in life without him, she had become the owner of a thriving internet business in the United States, and everything was going her way (oh, except for their foulmouthed, fully tattooed son). She was likely even less suited for the restrictions of marriage than Lin *san*. Being either a feminist or a male chauvinist would have made no difference, since some people just want a partner with that quality.

Emily had to have known that behind his bossy, impulsive style was a generous but lonely man.

The mind is willing, as the saying goes, the flesh is weak, but in his case, it was not necessarily limited to vigor. With one more person comes more worries, and that is exhausting.

Why hadn't he felt this way before?

He had a twinge of guilt but no regrets.

As he thought back, he realized he was not always able to intuit what was on her mind, likely because she was so different from all those worldlier women with their distinctive personalities.

As Lin sat at the Bösendorfer, he was hostage to a single thought: Only this piano knew his late wife's emotions before she married him.

From playing Schumann as a child and then Beethoven in her teens, from going abroad to returning home, from a double major to the violin, from being a student to becoming a teacher . . .

Did she commemorate the transition to becoming someone's wife on the piano keys?

Had it been hard to give up the dream of being a concert pianist?

Later, during the slack period while the music studio was being repurposed, Lin *san* frequently texted me, asking if I felt like playing the piano. I was welcome to do so any time.

If he happened to be there when I was practicing, he would drag a chair over and sit off to the side. He wasn't necessarily listening to me play, though. More likely, the music was a kind of therapy.

I can imagine how he might have started hearing things when he was alone in the house all day with the

Steinway. I wasn't surprised when he told me he thought he could hear it.

He was like an old piano, something he might not be conscious of.

Maybe that was why he thought he heard the piano. An instrument that no one played any more became his self-projection, whether he would admit it or not.

Sometimes we went to a pub, an old haunt, after locking up the studio.

The different setting seemed to put him at ease and gradually made him more talkative.

"This pub has been around for nearly twenty years," he said. "I worry about how long it will last, so I drop in whenever I can."

"Were you always alone back then?" I asked, trying to envision how he'd looked twenty years younger.

"I'd just gotten divorced when it opened. I'd come here with some drinking buddies and was in the habit of hanging out with them until I met Emily and we decided to get married."

He'd met these drinking buddies when he started his business. It helped to be acquainted with older men like a successful stock market trader, a bank general manager, an arms dealer, and a media tycoon, movers and shakers who could weather any political storm and survive a regime change.

Lin *san* never could figure out how well they knew each

other, though. At first it was a huge honor to be invited to their gatherings, but he soon realized that either they never talked about anything important or that the topics of their conversations never overlapped. Whenever there was a lull, someone would top off the glasses and propose a toast, "Bottoms up." It was the same every time. But as a latecomer, he had to sit patiently.

To them, Lin *san* was a promising business acquaintance worth knowing, as well as a good listener when they got together to drink. More importantly, being a generation younger, he was reliable, never failing to take them home when they were too drunk to drive.

"Emily didn't like them?"

"She wasn't—" He paused to weigh his words, as if the thoughts could burn his tongue. "You see, women have friends with whom they can share everything, but men can't. When men part ways, that's it, no feelings of loss. Don't you agree? Have you ever heard a man say to another man, 'I miss you'? Ha-ha-ha."

Why was that so funny. Haven't you read "A Letter to Yuan Weizhi" by Bai Juyi? I nearly blurted out. A habit I developed later on of holding back what I wanted to say to him might have had its origin in that moment.

"Why don't you ask your friends out?"

"They were good to be with back when we were all on top of the world. But now? No way."

*

He's older now than they were then. At some point, they stopped meeting in pubs or hotel bars and switched to a private room at a restaurant that specialized in Taiwanese cuisine. Nearly eighty now, they are still as competitive as ever. He knew that, because he'd gotten them all together forty-nine days—the seven sevens—after Emily's funeral. It was meant to announce his intention to pull himself together. It had been two years since they'd last met, so they asked how each other was doing, as usual. When it came to Lin, he couldn't even offer simple information in complete sentences. "Emily, pancreatic cancer, diagnosed six months ago, since she's gone, I ..."

He couldn't finish.

He'd expected them to offer condolences and encouragement, but he got virtually no reaction, as if he'd just commented on a traffic jam or mentioned a new restaurant. They simply went back to the conversation he'd interrupted.

It dawned on him that death was nothing new to these old men. They might not even have remembered who Emily was. His marriage was over so soon he couldn't even recall who among those old men had attended his wedding.

He could not say what he'd expected. He'd decided to have dinner with them precisely because personal matters never cropped up in their rambling conversations, hadn't he?

Midway through dinner, the oldest among them,

Mr. Zhao, the arms dealer, commented, "Coffins are for the dead, not for the old."

"Who died?" the man sitting next to Zhao asked.

"Lin's ex-wife."

"But they divorced a long time ago, didn't they?"

Lin *san* laughed despite himself when he talked about that dinner.

As we chatted, I realized he was not a grim, solemn man. I sometimes could not help but wonder what he was like when he was drunk. He'd likely been my age at the time.

Now he could no longer play the role of the youngest in the group. He might even feel older than they had at the time. When you reach a certain age, I discovered, your mental capacity doesn't always match your actual age. Everyone gets the same card that says "Old," and sixty is no different from eighty.

There was a time when he lamented things like this.

Upon his return to Taipei after an overseas business trip late one night, he was suddenly quite hungry. Only the pub would still be open at that hour, he reasoned. The owner always asked the kitchen to prepare some simple snacks for regulars. He was surprised to see Brother Zhang, whom everyone called Chairman, sitting alone in a corner.

"Why haven't you asked the others to join you?"

Brother Zhang smiled and mumbled a response: "Too much trouble."

Unsure what the man meant, he persisted, foolishly.

"Why not go to the hostess bar we went to last time? You can get a girl to drink with you. It's no fun drinking alone."

Lin *san* sat down to join Zhang, who, with little to say, was not acting like the "Chairman," invariably the loudest in the group. It became clear that these men had never been bosom buddies. His own presence, like kindling in a stove, had lifted their mood and made them talk and brag. They were spurred on with a younger, less experienced man in the audience. The older a man is, the more he cares about face. When suffering from loneliness, he can only hide out and be alone.

"An old man drinking alone is a sad sight," Lin *san* told me. "I'd just been liberated and was surrounded by plenty of pretty women, so naturally I didn't think that one day I'd be old."

"You're still a very desirable man, and there must be lots of women just waiting to hook up with you." This is what I usually said when I sensed that his spirits were low.

"Ha. Getting involved with a woman is the worst thing I could do now."

He brushed off the comment and explained that it wasn't because he was still in mourning or because he feared gossip. He just didn't have the energy for it, a surprise discovery. A man spends his whole life learning how to please women, only to be told that he doesn't understand them.

"What about you, young man?"

"Me? What about me?"

"What do you think?" Every time he raised the same question, I'd respond by taking off my cap to expose my baldness. "No looks, no money. I know where I stand. What else can I do?"

Luckily, he never persisted or pried when I feigned ignorance or gave him a nonanswer. He'd simply look at me with an expression that said he'd crossed more bridges than the number of roads I'd walked on. Then he'd snort, with his eyes half shut.

5

I FELT THE URGE to reveal everything to him on many occasions, but I wanted to keep from being overly sentimental.

I recall what a now-dead Nobel literature laureate once said:

"Anyone with enough experience can make up stories, but only those who truly understand the world have something meaningful to say."

Thinking about it now, that may define Lin *san* and me.

Filling him in on things would not have helped our relationship. I'd made a pact with myself, convinced that people like him would never understand what being a piano tuner meant to me.

There are some things people cannot grasp, no matter how carefully you explain them.

Like my earliest memory of the Steinway.

Like Emily's Steinway. Nothing was wrong with it; she was just unhappy.

Or like the opportunity I'd once had to lead a different life. If only I'd been able to forget the bewilderment and disappointment I'd felt on that hot summer day when inexplicably I thought that snow had fallen.

Maybe it had to do with what happened later, maybe not. I must continue with my narration, or I'll never have my answer.

Who keeps banging out those splintered notes in that indistinct world?

Ms. Chiu did not ask me why I quit the piano. And we lost touch after that.

I failed my physical exam, the first hurdle to acceptance in a military academy, because I was underweight. I thus dodged the life Father had planned for me. At the age of sixteen, I began working in the day and attending a business vocational school at night.

Until the summer before my junior year in high school.

I was changing out of my work clothes before racing off to school for the finals when Ms. Chiu called me. She said she wanted to introduce me to a former classmate from her middle school music class. *What? Oh, sure.* I had no idea why she arranged the meeting.

Feeling guilty and uneasy, I went to meet them, not knowing what awaited me. I found the scene curious the moment I sat down: how could she and the promising young man look so natural together?

I could tell from her eyes that she admired, even adored the man, who turned out to be an internationally renowned pianist who had returned to Taiwan for a stint as a visiting professor at a certain university. What he had accomplished was obviously a dream beyond her reach at this stage. How many young men and women in music classes still lived for that dream? Why was she still single? They looked to be a perfect match.

My thoughts were running wild.

After the obligatory small talk to break the ice, she cut to the chase: "You've wasted enough time. Don't you ever think about your future?"

What did she mean by "wasting time"? Was I wasting my talent? Or was I some deadbeat who had been born with a silver spoon in his mouth? I felt like arguing with her. Frankly, even now I don't get what she was driving at with those words.

"Please give it some serious thought. There isn't much time left, but I believe you can do it if you want to."

Biting down on my lip, I recalled that afternoon when we'd linked pinkies. "Why should I try to get into a college music department?" It took me a long time to protest softly.

"You have too much pride. I know you better than you know yourself. You've been waiting for this day, actually, to prove you don't have to travel the path others take. They'll remember how special you are. In one semester you can outshine others who struggle for five, six years."

While she continued with her motivational speech, I noticed that the gaze from beside her remained pensive and on my hands.

She left so the pianist and I could talk alone.

When he asked to hear something from me, I played Rachmaninoff's "Song Without Words." He asked why I'd picked the piece. I looked at him and shrugged, but then for some reason that made me mad. "Because it's written for a soprano, and I think that's a mistake."

To my surprise, he laughed at my reply. Behind his gold-rimmed glasses was the frank and open gaze of a guileless young man, something I hadn't seen for a while.

"What's on your mind when you play the piece?"

"Snow," I said.

"Have you ever seen snow?"

"No."

"Then why snow?"

I remember I lowered my head, afraid to look him in the eye, feeling I was about to cry for no reason. I could not make it clear that to me it was like walking amid swirling snow, even though I'd never seen any.

I had trouble finding the words. "Maybe it wasn't snow," I said. "Just a feeling that something was falling all around me."

He mulled my answer over.

"The thing you can't describe," he continued, "is time. Music lets us hear time pass and it lets us hear our shadows."

I looked up in surprise and saw him studying me.

I'd known only that I had superior equipment, but until that day no one had told me that music isn't in the piano, it's in my shadow.

He also said that everyone is born with a resonating formula, which some will look for in a musical instrument, others in singing. Those who are luckiest can find, in this vast world, a vibration that can awaken the resonance with their past, present, and future.

It can be something called love or it can be trust. What we hear when we listen to someone play the piano is less the music than the passing of notes, which are always in the present, never to be repeated.

"Everyone can be touched by Debussy or Bach, including the loneliest, the most impoverished, even the dying, because their music is our shared origin and destination," he said.

Yes, I'll never forget what he said to me that day.

Ever since then, I keep asking myself what the New York pianist saw in me. A willful, shiftless, conceited genius who will never amount to much. I was sure he'd seen through me.

Unlike Ms. Chiu, he did not have high expectations for me, though I doubt that even she knew what she hoped to see in me. Could it simply have been that she couldn't get over how she had misjudged me?

The pianist spent that summer in his Taipei childhood home.

Not a villa on Yangmingshan or a luxury high-rise in a district favored by the cultural elite. It was an old-style alley structure in a neighborhood once known for its bar scene. With peeling walls, it was a far cry from the quarters reserved for him in the university guesthouse.

He said he had to be home because he could not play on an unfamiliar piano.

A magnificent Steinway sitting in a dark, old house amid unusual surroundings makes for a disjointed sight, which, when I think about it, gives me an eerie, surreal feeling.

"The piano was the one expensive gift from my father. I never took any money from him to study abroad, since I had a full scholarship," he said.

"Do you know what I miss most about this old house of ours? The area had a bustling nightlife when I was a kid, so I didn't have to worry about disturbing the neighbors when I practiced. They made more noise than I did."

Maybe encounters between some people can occur only in a certain era.

Back in those poverty-ridden days, owning classical music in original LPs was a rare luxury.

Ms. Chiu was pleased when I took her advice to study with the pianist. She never knew that we spent most of each lesson listening to his collection of vinyl LPs, a treasured experience.

At the time, we lived in a closed society, with scant flow of information.

Rachmaninoff had been dead for nearly half a century, and the pianists familiar to most students in Taiwan were still Rubinstein and Horowitz. Thanks to years of an anti-Communist, anti-Soviet Cold War, many Soviet pianists had been banned for years by their own government from going abroad, and they remained a taboo to us in Taiwan, even after they began to earn high praise in the West.

Years have gone by, and yet I'm always taken back to that summer whenever I hear the Soviet pianist Sviatoslav Richter play and am reminded of the first time the pianist played a live recording for me.

Under Richter's fingers, Schubert's Piano Sonata No. 18 in G major, D. 894, was graceful and unpredictable, so different from the reserved, placid style of other renditions. I still recall that the air seemed infused with a solitude unique to the cold country of the north.

Richter had no formal musical education in his youth. Then, when he was twenty, Heinrich Neuhaus, a piano teacher at the Moscow Conservatory, discovered his talent and made a personal exception by taking him on as a student.

*

I listened quietly as the pianist told me about Richter.

Richter won the Stalin Prize in 1949, which afforded him the opportunity to give concerts abroad. In the beginning, he was allowed to play only in China and Eastern European countries. His first US concert occurred in 1960, and he took the Western music world by storm.

But he did not like America, and he disliked foreign concert tours. He preferred traveling domestically, riding a train through Siberia and getting off whenever he saw a scenic little town to perform for the locals. What we heard from him was mostly live concert performances, since he was not a big fan of recording studios.

Pay attention to how he mastered the brief tranquil moments between notes.

Never forget that the silent portions are part of the music.

Many pianists can be majestic and impassioned when they play, but only Richter could interpret the lightness and quietude of piano notes so flawlessly.

Years later, when I started tutoring students, I followed the way the pianist had inspired me and listened to my favorite CDs with the students. But I was usually rewarded with criticism and complaints from parents who thought I was loafing on the job instead of making their children practice in order to meet their expected progress. Some fired me without hesitation. Piano tutoring is the easiest way for a music student to support himself, and yet I was often found unsuitable for the job, a real predicament.

Maybe I simply didn't know how to teach based on each student's ability and needs.

With only one semester of rigorous practice, I was admitted to a music department when others had to struggle for five or six years preparing to get in. How would I understand the obstacles others faced?

The pianist did not completely ignore Ms. Chiu's request and would suddenly be strict with me, especially after he finished his evaluation workshop every month. But his rigor never lasted a week.

"Even if you didn't want to get into a music department, you should at least have the experience of playing a fine piano, don't you think?" It was hard to argue against the reason he used to get me to practice. "I've personally asked a specialist to come all the way from Austria to tune it for me."

He had worked for years with the only tuner who knew what he needed. Before every concert, he would be anxious about which piano to use, and in the end, he sought help from this particular tuner to put his mind at ease.

I still recall how I felt the first time I played the famous and very expensive Steinway, adjusted by a world-renowned tuner. Thinking back to my surprise, joy, and helplessness at that moment still makes me laugh.

"I can't really describe the timbre I hear," he said. "The frequency and layered vibrations alone can take me to a magical realm that makes me feel safe and yet a bit sad."

I said I knew what he meant.

His mother stopped by one day. A woman in her late fifties, she still wore heavy makeup and had unruly, permed hair, dyed a chestnut red. She was amiable as she brought out some presliced cake and invited us to take a break and enjoy the snack. Yet, hidden in the smile was a fierce snobbishness and adroitness in social interactions that even her superficial geniality could not hide.

"Where do you live, young man? Who did you study with before this? Will you be going abroad?"

After the string of questions, she apparently lost interest in me and gave her son a quick, reproachful glance, as if to ask where he'd picked up this piece of goods? Shamefaced, I sat woodenly, staring at the half-eaten cake on my plate until he urged his mother to leave.

An internationally renowned pianist with a mother whose background as a working girl was plain to see would be fodder for today's paparazzi, a salacious headline story in the making, claiming the pianist was probably the illegitimate child of a certain politician.

I'd thought he had the same sort of problems as a prodigy that I did until he told me that he'd worked very hard for his mother's sake.

"As for so-called genius," he said, "some simply have

more advanced development in nerve cells, which at a certain age will slow down to be like everyone else." While overseas, he had seen too many concert pianists of his age destroyed by the frightful realization that their genius had waned.

"But I've never given a thought to becoming a concert pianist," I said.

"That's why I agreed to let you play here." He never failed to quiet me.

Though, at first, I didn't understand his fear.

At thirty-four, he was still young enough to joke childishly with me, a seventeen-year old. But for a rising star who had been in the musical spotlight for ten years, he would have to be considered over the hill, since he hadn't yet had a breakthrough.

He had never played with the Berlin Philharmonic or Zubin Mehta, nor had he ever signed a million-dollar recording contract. More and more invitations came from music festivals that were lively but lacked prestige.

He had been drifting alone overseas for too long, with nothing in his life but his agent and his audience. Later I learned that he had agreed to the semester-long visiting position in Taiwan because he was manic depressive and needed a rest.

Likely he wasn't all that impressed by my special talent.

Likely he just needed someone by him as he recovered, which gave me the opportunity to share his Steinway.

Could he not know how fond Ms. Chiu was of him? He'd agreed to take me on perhaps as an apology for letting her down.

Compared with facing the unknown of each concert alone on stage, I think, it's a happier life being the most trusted, most dependable behind-the-scene person.

Not to be an accompanist or a study companion, but to be someone like a piano tuner by a pianist's side.

It was a time when nothing needed to be said, something I didn't realize until years later, when it turned out to be the quiet before the fin-de-siècle storm.

Once, before I walked into the living room for my lesson, I heard some very loud music and knew right away it was Bach's *Goldberg Variations*.

"Wow, terrific. Who's playing?"

I expressed my admiration with delight, I recall, thinking he had come up with another test for me. I was about to show off my ability to appreciate music when he retorted coolly and listlessly from his sofa seat.

"You think so?"

Picking up the LP sleeve, I pretended to read it, not daring to say another word. I was so ignorant back then I didn't know it was the mad genius Glenn Gould, a Canadian who had died at the young age of fifty; nor did I know that he had been such an influential pianist in the West that he had shaken up the music world. On this day, the pianist was playing the LP that had made Gould's fame.

A rare piano genius with extraordinary skill, Gould had refused to play at concerts after he became famous, insisting that the best music could be made only in a recording studio, not a concert hall. He'd willingly play a piece twenty times in a recording studio until he was happy with the result, not in the least minding modifications or editing.

Gould was contemptuous of the high prices charged at concerts, calling it a privilege of the elite. He wanted to offer his music at an affordable price to more people.

He even made the unprecedented move of recording background noise, including himself humming along as he played.

He spent a great deal of time in front of a TV set. Though someone who never answered the phone, he was given to calling friends to share nagging worries about his health.

Three decades and more have passed since his death, but people still talk about his unusual behavior, publishing books about him, some of which deviate from music and instead examine temporal and hypothetical concerns as well as the architectural designs of concert halls, the operation and organization of concerts, media, bureaucracy, the flow of capital, and other varied subjects. Gould remains a controversial figure among music fans.

Looking back now, we can see that he'd made one

accurate prediction: the traditional way we receive and appreciate music would undergo a fundamental change.

Back at a time when the digital downloading of music was still a sci-fi fantasy, on one end of the spectrum there was Richter, who insisted on live performances and rejected studio recordings. On the other was Glenn Gould, who believed that music was the focus and that it didn't matter if a piece was not completed in one sitting.

It was then that I forgot myself and argued with the pianist, probably out of a rebellious streak.

"Didn't you tell me Richter's stepfather told him about his mother's death, with no forewarning, as he was about to go on stage at his first Vienna concert? By performing badly, he suffered relentless criticism from music critics, with expressions like shattered myth and dead legend. Why should he have been subjected to that kind of humiliation? Musicians are human beings, they have emotions. Why can't they lose control sometimes?"

"Musicians don't live for the critics. Those people are nothing but failed musicians and malicious bastards. They pretend to be experts, making a big show out of nothing, and content themselves with the pay they earn for their reviews. With no dreams or creativity, they are self-satisfied, pleased with the title 'critic.' Even if they all died tomorrow, music would not be affected one iota, and that's the truth."

This was the first time I'd seen him so angry he lost control. It was not easy imagining the kind of pressure he'd been under during those years. He paused before getting up to walk to the turntable. I didn't dare say another word, as Gould's music filled the room, so splendid, so precise, one high point after another.

The pianist did not speak until the record stopped.

"You're right. When you walk onto the stage, you face a situation that's completely beyond your control. A pianist can only focus on his dialogue with the piano. Isn't life the same? Overcome the demons in your heart and venture out with the first step."

He continued to talk about Richter's later years, when his eyesight failed. The strong stage lights were too much for him, so they were doused, leaving only a tiny light on the piano. It didn't matter if his audience was peasants or the rich and mighty, he played on, a lone figure in semidarkness.

"Besides, he'd picked the piece for his deathbed. It would be a Schubert piano sonata. In the end, it isn't important if one is a concert pianist or not. What matters most is to have something that brings you peace, free of regrets, when you reach the end of your life's journey."

No one could have predicted that the pianist himself would leave the world before lonely, sad Richter. I was only seventeen, not an age at which someone can know about death.

What occurred to me at the time was the story of Schubert, the unlucky composer.

Barely five feet tall, not particularly good-looking, with thinning hair, and neurotic, he was poor and underappreciated throughout his life. He was never lucky in love and yet contracted syphilis during one of his rare nights with a woman.

It is hard to imagine the scale of misfortune Schubert suffered. He was forever on the brink of a spiritual abyss, like a wandering ghost. Dead at the age of thirty, he wasn't recognized for his talent, unlike Chopin and Liszt, who both enjoyed many more romantic encounters than he.

Luckily, he had his music. He completed nine symphonies, twenty-one piano sonatas, and countless songs and pieces of chamber music.

Was it enough to have music? Or could it be that he was never after fame? He was able to leave behind so much because of the emptiness and the unfulfilled desire and need for love.

What if he had given up his quest for love?

I turned to look at Gould's picture on the album cover. A gaunt, bald man with a hunched back and protruding ears, Gould even crossed his leg when he played. Then I said something that surprised even me.

"Say, maybe what he gave up on wasn't concerts but a kind of waiting, like a means of withdrawal. He stopped playing concerts to declare a severance from what he loved most. Do you think that's possible?"

I still recall the surprised, pained look in his eyes when he heard what I had blurted out without thinking.

I was prophetic without meaning to. When it was all over, I finally understood his internal struggle and the scourge that plagued his generation.

Ms. Chiu and I never broached the subject of the pianist's death, so I knew only that he had come down with "a strange illness" in the early 1990s. Later, she and I even tried to ignore his lamentable past.

When I learned of Richter's death in 1997, I was beset by a myriad of complex emotions that are hard to describe. To me, Richter wasn't the only one who'd died; the aura of classical music dimmed when the last master of the twentieth century was gone. Everything was commercialized, and musicians began playing popular music; vinyl went out of fashion, and even cassette tapes were replaced by compact discs.

I'd owned the pianist's music only on cassettes. It was no longer hard to find Richter's music on CD, but I could not replace those tapes when they wore out. Within a few years of his death, the pianist could not be found in the world of digital music.

I made a special trip to visit the pianist's childhood home, but the row of old houses in the alley had been razed.

Disappointment aside, I could not stop thinking about the splendid piano in his old place.

When he finished his visiting professorship and returned to New York, I already had a feeling he would never come back. Yet I was foolish enough to believe the piano would stay, and that would be enough for me. I did not expect that everything that had happened that year would disappear, like snow in the summer, vanishing without a trace.

So what happened to the piano?

As a narrator, what else do I have to reveal about myself?

I mean, except for the fact that I was a musical genius?

6

W HEN DEBUSSY'S EVOCATIVE "Arabesque No. 1" came to an end, the pianist held his hands aloft for three seconds, like a pair of swans gliding across the lake surface before coming ashore.

A quarter of a century later, the youth finally had another chance to sit at a Steinway and hear the keys murmur dreamily under his fingers. For a brief moment, the young man from twenty-five years earlier reappeared in the reflection on the piano's black walnut body, but faded away with the last note.

I sat quietly for a few seconds, expecting to hear the pianist say "excellent." Instead, I was rewarded with brief applause from the hands of Lin *san*, who had walked into the living room at some point.

As if awakening from a dream, I exhaled deeply.

The Steinway he gave his wife was not in the antique class, but I estimated it would still have cost at least three million New Taiwan dollars.

I should not have accepted his offer to come play here. But he said otherwise he'd have to make a special trip to the music studio to unlock the door for me. If he'd found me completely trustworthy, he could have given me a set of keys, but he preferred having me as a frequent visitor at his home.

I don't know which would have been less awkward.

In the beginning, I even wondered if he'd made a discovery.

If his real purpose was to ask me about Emily, how long could I maintain my taciturn indifference?

"Are you serious?" I turned to look at Lin *san* after his question. "What led to this sudden decision to take up the piano?"

"I've always wanted to learn to play but never carried through with it. The older one gets, the harder it is to face making a fool of oneself, and the more difficult the first step."

"What changed?"

I flipped through the sheet music on the shelf but failed to find anything useful for beginners.

"I just felt you'd be a good teacher."

That's just the way Lin *san* talked. The passive tone carried a strong desire to own the conversation.

I didn't see it at first, as his kind gestures exceeded my expectation. Sympathy and guilt led me to accept all his invitations. I even went with him to the French restaurant where he and Emily first met. Without knowing it, I became an audience of one to his grieving process.

If only he could see how awkward it was for me to sit across from him. If Emily's spirit were nearby, would she be as amused and yet annoyed as I was?

I guess that, in the beginning, I could have chosen to distance myself, owing to apprehensive feelings that were increasingly hard to conceal. But his loneliness, his sense of loss, and his lackluster marriage to Emily seemed to have become, for me, an inescapable responsibility.

When the past reared its head out of the blue, I experienced a feeling that I somehow owed the man an apology.

I can't recall how often I'd been there to tune the piano for Emily, but this time it was a hot summer afternoon.

Suddenly, I was the only one inside and the house grew quiet.

Looking through the French doors, I saw Emily and a guest who had dropped by in conversation beneath the plane tree. She seemed to be avoiding me. The visitor, a tall, trim man with a ponytail, looked to be a younger man. I saw he had the slender, up-slanting, single-fold eyes that Westerners find so attractive.

An image that had been buried deep for so long floated to the surface that afternoon.

Shortly before his return to New York, the pianist had agreed to a recital. If he were to add a four-handed duet to the program, he said, would the young man be willing to join him up on the stage?

The young man laughed and said he wouldn't dream of it.

"No? That's only because you don't have any decent clothes," the pianist said, mocking the young man as usual. "We'll have something made for you. We'll do it."

Despite what he'd said, the young man's heart nearly burst over the promise and the excitement. He was keyed up not because of the many VIPs who would be in the audience, but because of the image of him, also in a tuxedo with a bow tie, sitting shoulder to shoulder with the pianist.

Now, what I saw was Emily under the tree, facing away. At some point, her hair had come undone and was hanging loose. Ponytail was running his fingers through it.

On a similarly hot summer afternoon, the abrupt appearance of a blond man with blue eyes broke the promise of a four-handed piano piece, which was relegated to the young man's imagination.

The pianist was speaking French with the visitor as they went to his room, leaving the young man to sit alone at the piano. Old and worn, the door of the room could not be shut snugly and slid open just enough for a pair of eyes to look in, unnoticed by the two inside. The blond man was holding the pianist tightly in his arms, their lips like two cicadas finding each other after a summer-long search and hurrying to mate before the season was over.

Later I said to Emily, "I saw you." She was stunned and then began to sob.

I reached over to lift up her chin.

Many people have commented on my hands; they're well-structured and proportioned, with long fingers. Even the pianist once said they were the hands of a born pianist. I had nothing to offer the sobbing woman, except that beautiful miracle on my person.

But that did not stop Emily from reacting as if violated; she jerked her face around and pushed my hand away.

How does one separate sympathy from feelings of guilt?

Why does betrayal come so easily to some people?

I was not the pianist's partner in the four-hand duet. The music world was thrilled to have the blond young man, also a concert pianist, as the mystery guest at that night's performance, an event that was widely talked about. It could never have been me. Why had I been so clueless? It wasn't even betrayal, strictly speaking, just something said in jest that I mistook as real. I'd already decided to give up the piano and knew it would have made no difference, and yet I let myself once again—

The oblivious older man was still mired in loneliness and self-reproach in the wake of his wife's death. He could open his heart only to his late wife's piano tuner, a musical genius with no chance of getting closer to his wife, an odd-ball trying to blackmail her for attention, a flawed object ignored by those inflicting harm.

I knew I had to keep everything to myself.

All these years, I'd been used to being the lonely black key, while the white keys seemed to exist forever beyond the reach of my fingertips.

Helplessly, I watched the young man in my memory be abandoned by the pianist.

In my recollection, he clenched his fist, a screw held between two fingers. With his eyes closed, he could only hear the screw leaving a long, screech on the Steinway's silken body.

Then he ran out in tears, tearing down the alley as if his life depended on it. He knew no one would notice his absence and come looking for him. He just had to keep running.

That was all I thought I could do, run with no end, run until I didn't know where I was, until Lin *san* gave me a chance to sit at a Steinway again and hear my heart beat.

I'd long since quit making a living by tutoring, let alone

teach the man before me. So I made an excuse about a busy tuning schedule but left it at that, for fear that he would persist with more questions. He cocked his head and mulled my reply over, adopting a heavy tone when he spoke again.

"If I don't learn to play, this piano will sit idle, for no one would touch it again."

It will wind up sitting idle sooner or later.

It's hard to say how quickly a piano that isn't played will deteriorate, even if it is regularly tuned.

But I didn't think he was serious about learning to play. There seemed to be layers of meaning in his comment, impossible to make sense of at first.

I instinctively thought he'd wanted to sell the Steinway along with the others in the studio, for he'd asked if I knew any secondhand dealers and how much I thought each piano was worth.

When I didn't respond right away, he followed up with a new idea.

"Piano tuning alone cannot produce a stable income, I imagine. And the hourly rate is far lower than giving music lessons. The director told me that Emily thought you were a pretty good pianist. Why don't you start teaching here? You've all the pianos you would need."

*

Looking up, I thought I could see two figures embracing under the plane tree through the French doors.

I've never felt the need for friends, so it's impossible for me to say if betrayal is the inescapable noise in the resonance between people.

The seven-year-old boy and twenty-four-year-old Ms. Chiu. The seventeen-year-old and the thirty-four-year-old pianist. The forty-three-year-old and the nearly sixty-year-old Lin *san*.

The same age difference repeated over and over, like the wheel of samsara.

Or like two keys on a piano, the same distance between them but with dissimilar intervals, creating altogether different vibrations and resonance.

If one senses loneliness and despair from the resonance between sixty and eighty, could that be caused by a long-needed tuning? Which of the repeated intervals is closest to Pythagoras's hypothesis on harmony?

Someone will always be hurt.

Is it because everyone, except for the musical genius, knows how to calculate risks?

Lin *san* asked me to be present when the secondhand instrument wholesaler came to the studio for an estimate. He didn't need me to tell him what result he could expect; the offering price alone was chilling enough.

"Are these all you've got? That's it?" The man looked at me rather than at Lin, as if he could read minds.

I avoided Lin *san*'s eyes.

Even after turning down the offer to teach on Emily's Steinway, I continued to play it.

I might be thinking that I could stop an indescribable sense of loss slowly inching toward me if I didn't let the Steinway fall into disuse. It had been years since I'd been so engrossed in anything; I spent more and more time playing, since I no longer had to worry about taking up someone else's time.

Except that I hadn't been to the pub with Lin *san* for a couple of weeks. All we had left were unavoidable greetings and polite small talk. One day, when we were alone in the room, I decided to break the ice after a brief hesitation.

"How, how have you been?"

He didn't reply as he went to lock up the practice rooms.

It had reached the stage where he'd invited someone over for an estimate.

Obviously, he would not accept my explanation that teaching the piano wasn't what I wanted in my life at the moment. I'd always been here just to tune and keep the pianos in good shape; it had never been a concern of mine who they belonged to.

Why should it be my responsibility where the pianos ended up? Why would he think I'd agree to offer piano lessons in his house?

After I finished playing Liszt's "Un Sospiro" on the Bösendorfer, I sensed him nearby, waiting to lock up the last room.

His dejected look gave me the feeling that he was ready to let go. When he locked up this time, I might not have another chance to play this piano.

And we might not have any more contact after this, since he had once said that when a friendship between two men ended, that was it.

But Emily wouldn't be gone just like that.

I wavered when I thought of the secret I had to continue keeping. Unless he was ready to give up the Steinway?

I helped him straighten up before he locked up the room. I realized we both hesitated when we reached the entrance. Neither wanted to be the first to push open the door.

"Where are you going now?" he asked me.

"I'm going to buy some sheet music."

Over those years, I'd never stopped listening to Richter's renditions of Schubert's piano sonatas, on CD and then on an iPod, be it No. 18, D. 894 or No. 12, D. 960. But I never thought of including them in the pieces I played.

Schumann, maybe. Liszt and Chopin, I'd worked hard on these when preparing for college admission. Debussy and Rachmaninoff, my all-time favorites. But Schubert, I skirted all these years, intentionally or not.

Maybe subconsciously I was scared off by Schubert's life; more likely, however, Richter's performance was simply too good, too intimidating, and I'd been avoiding the challenge.

Surprisingly, my confidence got a boost after practicing at Lin's house over those days, and I finally decided to give it a try.

Even more surprising to me was that Lin *san*, the husband of a musician, had never been to a sheet music store.

An established shop located in the old section of the city's West Gate area, it had been in business for fifty years and was much more appealing to me than the faddish, artiste boutiques shaped by famous interior designers. In a space like that, a young man trying hard to act like an artist was a common sight.

You could tell it was a dancer by the long scarf, the loose cotton-linen pants, and the frosty look. An actor, on the other hand, would be intentionally understated, dressed in old jeans and sneakers, appearing to be in a hurry, but not so rushed as to ignore the gazes around them.

Then there were the young women who looked older than their age because of the high heels and chignons, or young men dressed all in black, though apparently without gang connections. If they were holding a bouquet of flowers, they had to be members of a chorus or a chamber music group, for that was the standard post-performance look.

Luckily, they did not normally show up at my favorite old shop.

It was in an ancient building, a relic from the Japanese colonial era, with steep, narrow stairs and no landing. After reaching the third floor, I opened the door and turned to see the surprised look on Lin *san's* face, just as I'd expected.

An accidental shopper could not possibly tell, at first glance, what kind of place this was. The walls were lined, from top to bottom, with glass-fronted wooden drawers; each drawer was custom made, long and thin, the exact size for opened sheet music. Each musical note waited quietly in its drawer.

It was like a sutra storage in a temple or a medical lab with a long history. What was stored in the tiny compartments, it would seem, was not sheet music, but the DNA of celebrated composers. Each folio was stored and retrieved by human hands. When one of the flat drawers was pulled out, you could see and smell the wood grain, as well as the paper pulp unique to printed musical notes. Here you would not find bound volumes of sheet music, only loose leaves. Everyone was careful when pulling out the drawers, afraid of creasing, damaging, or dirtying the pages.

Lin *san* circled the shop quietly and stopped behind me at some point to watch me retrieve sheets of Schubert's music.

"So, where will you practice these once I sell the Steinway?" he said softly after a while.

At that moment I thought he'd made up his mind, but I also detected something else.

Actually, I'd already found a solution for the music studio.

I forced myself to say nothing, not wanting to overstep my status as a tuner. I thought I'd be different from all those other people in his life and did not want him to misunderstand me. In fact, I was just like them, unable to be content with our brief encounter without further expectations.

Something must have happened at that moment, for I recall that I croaked out a response once I'd regained my composure.

"Whether you make money or not isn't important. The key is, not only can you hold on to Ms. Chen's pianos, but you can also keep the music studio. The space is large enough to contain ten pianos. Even though there will be no music lessons, at least it'll be a music-related business."

7

PIANO MANUFACTURING TECHNIQUES reached new heights by the end of the nineteenth century. In New York City, the sale of pianos was a popular trade, like the stock market on Wall Street, the theaters on Broadway, or newspaper publications.

More than a hundred and seventy piano factories were concentrated in the city. Tens of thousands of pianos under several hundred brands were made and sold here in New York.

After reaching their peak in the 1920s, piano sales in New York started going downhill, and the slide continued unabated. The advancement of recording technology, coupled with wireless radio broadcasts, upended the convention that a piano could be found wherever there was music, which had stood for centuries. Going to a concert hall and sitting properly for a performance was too much of a luxury, so pianists walked into recording studios.

By the 1980s, a mere five manufacturers remained in business all across America, and Steinway was the only company in New York still making pianos.

On the other hand, even if a great many people still wanted pianos, there weren't enough trees to cut down; the raw material for making pianos grew scarce and harder to obtain.

Except for famous instruments that were painstakingly maintained, most pianos ended up being disassembled, their components reused on repairable pianos. What could not be salvaged would be recycled as scrap. New York ceased to be the capital of the piano world, but a reversal of fortunes some years later turned the city into a center of piano reconstruction and secondhand retail.

Would the concept of a soul still be valid when a piano was reconstructed?

I would say, from a professional point of view, that age was not an issue. If there were indeed a soul, then it would be released only after a spell was broken during tuning; otherwise, it would be imprisoned forever.

It was past ten at night when we arrived at the Carlyle Hotel not far from Central Park. Lin *san*, who hadn't slept on the twenty-hour flight, looked utterly exhausted. After a hurried good-night, we went to our facing rooms.

I dozed off fully dressed, and when I awoke some time later, the digital clock on the bedside table told me it was past midnight. Opening my suitcase, I took out a newly purchased down jacket, put it on, and walked out of the hotel for an aimless stroll on the deserted streets.

Before setting off, neither of us knew what changes the fateful appointment might bring. Lin *san* had asked how I'd come upon the idea of trading in secondhand pianos. I was honest with him, saying that for years I'd been chatting online with piano fans around the globe. I knew something about pianos, though I was just an armchair strategist.

Without further comment, he said only, "Then we should get more secondhand pianos."

He made flight and hotel reservations before I had a chance to do more homework.

Was it because of Emily or an overestimation of my own ability I couldn't say. I'd thought I would never have a chance to visit New York, so walking down Fifth Avenue felt unreal.

It was an early morning weekday at the beginning of November, and the streets were quiet except for street sweepers and speeding yellow cabs. The taxis whizzed by, rushing somewhere, as if afraid of missing out on something. I had to wonder if there were secret spots unmarked on the city map, unknown to visitors.

In a Manhattan devoid of pedestrians, dry, cold winds

were especially gusty. Before I knew it, I was standing at the southern tip of Fifth Avenue, by the arch at Washington Square.

I knew the surrounding buildings were part of the NYU campus.

This was where, years ago, the sixteen-year-old pianist had stepped onto his stage.

At twenty-two, he had his first major recital at Lincoln Center's Alice Tully Hall. The *New York Times* published a rave review the next day, thus changing a young concert pianist's life forever.

Many musical geniuses in their teens or early twenties already had their tickets to conquer this city.

As for someone coming for the first time in his forties, he would only be reminded of the points that had expired, no longer to be redeemed.

On that early morning in Washington Square, I realized, for the first time, that I'd already been in the world longer than he had. Yet every time I thought of him, I could not help looking up like a child, as if waiting for his approval.

I'd only enjoyed his stage performances on the videos he'd brought back; I'd never been in the audience when he played. They were Betamax tapes that quickly went out of use, and it never occurred to me to make copies.

I didn't even make it to his final performance. Surprisingly, after so many years, I still recalled what he'd told me about New York.

I should have known that when I was in the pianist's other hometown, the stage that had once embraced him, I would be mired in a series of puzzling, troubling "what-ifs."

If we had kept up correspondence, I might have learned about his former Manhattan residence. To be sure, this was idle thinking that would lead nowhere, for he had been dead nearly twenty-five years.

But what if the French musician still lived there?

Had they ever lived together? Was the Frenchman at his side when he died?

I had no interest in understanding a romantic relationship between two men; what I wanted to know was, had the Steinway I'd defaced been shipped to New York?

Had the Frenchman taken possession of the piano after his death? If I knew where he lived, would I have the courage to go see him?

If, only if, when the door opened, I realized I'd been misinformed, as the pianist appeared in front of me, a middle-aged man, in his sixties now, putting on weight. He'd decided to restart his life, live in permanent obscurity. . . .

We headed south on Broadway the next morning after breakfast.

On the west side of Midtown Manhattan, there were more than a dozen secondhand piano stores and restoration factories in addition to the famous Steinway and Petrof showrooms. With his silver hair and Armani suits, when we walked in, the clerks invariably assumed that Lin *san* was an important musician from some Asian country.

No one noticed me trailing behind, baseball cap pressed down over my forehead. I had to laugh privately at the surprised and embarrassed looks on their faces when they saw me sit down to try out an instrument.

At the fourth shop we were greeted by a young Asian woman. She switched to Mandarin when she heard us commenting on an exquisite Mason & Hamlin piano that looked like an expensive piece of furniture. She asked if we were from Taiwan.

"You can call me Xiao Zhang." She told us she was from Beijing and had recently received her PhD in music from Julliard. Lin *san* and I exchanged smiles. She asked why.

"You're the third one today with a degree from Julliard," I told her.

"What other shops have you visited? Have you met Raymond? He's from Argentina, a classmate of mine, actually." She wasn't bothered and actually laughed at my comment. "New York isn't just choked with actors waiting for auditions. There are also legions of musicians striving to become concert pianists."

She sat down to play a piece for us. Not half-bad. The problem was with the Grotrian. It had the same problem as all the secondhand pianos I'd played in other shops; the tuner had gone overboard in highlighting its loud, clear qualities.

*

"So, what kind of piano have you been playing, Mr. Lin?"

He looked stumped by the question, so I stepped in and told her it was a Steinway. She had the same reaction he had.

"So, what's wrong? Why do you want a new piano?"

"It's not for me," he said. "It's for him."

This is how he dodged the issue, a spur-of-the-moment response—he was not about to reveal his business plan—but my ears rang, for a brief hallucinatory moment at least, over the ridiculous idea of someone offering to buy me a piano.

Zhang's expression told me she was pondering the price range of pianos to recommend. Or maybe she was even more confused about someone gifting a yahoo like me a piano.

Neither of us said a word, so she led me over to a glossy black concert grand with "Ritmüller" above the keyboard. Somewhat dubious, I sat down to play some Chopin.

"What do you think? Not bad, hm?" She pointed to the price tag on the stand, "Brand new. And only ten thousand US."

I told her I'd never heard of the brand.

"Made in China!" She was brimming with pride. "The factory is in Guangzhou. They can produce five hundred a day. In recent years, China has made tremendous progress in the quality of their pianos. They're low cost, so the whole piano market is forced to lower their prices to keep up with the competition."

In her eyes I was only good enough to play a piano like that.

After our three-day research ended, over dinner Lin *san* asked what I thought. Some of the pianos had mild defects, which, consciously or not, I exaggerated, adding that there must be plenty of dark secrets in a business I'd viewed too simply.

A waiter in ethnic costume brought our food with a smile. I'd seen the Russian Tea Room, with its red walls, only in Woody Allen's movies. I never imagined I'd one day be a guest at the famed New York restaurant.

"I've been in business most of my life, and I've seen every unscrupulous business type there is." I was surprised he hadn't lost heart. He laid a napkin across his lap and held up his wine glass. "I actually find it interesting that there are so many graduates of a famous music school selling pianos."

"That's why I don't want to teach. Too many of them want to be concert pianists. Maybe piano manufacturing has already been replaced by a musician assembly line."

"People wake up from a dream eventually, don't you think? Too much competition in the art world makes it hard to reach the top. I'm just a businessman who's familiar only with capital and profits, so I don't really know what their dreams are all about. Maybe they've seen too many Hollywood movies."

I could not and would not rebuke him. He could never understand what all-in meant to someone with little left in life.

"I know this is just me talking, but in my view stubborn people too often miss opportunities that are out there. Sometimes, people turn stubborn out of fear. Trading in secondhand pianos may be one of those opportunities you and I should seize. You might turn out to be a good partner. You might have a good head for business, but you just don't know it, not yet. If only we'd met earlier through Emily . . . Here, a toast to our future joint endeavor."

I raised my glass of red wine to toast, if not that, at least the emotional comment.

In fact, he hadn't let on that he'd decided to turn the music studio into a secondhand piano salesroom. He had, however, started paying my salary and now even called me his partner.

At first, I was surprised and flattered by the elevated treatment, but on second thought, who else could have taken him along on tuning trips or taught him piano construction and the special traits of manufacturers?

Who had helped him learn online about secondhand piano sales outside Taiwan and names unfamiliar to Taiwanese? Who else apprised him of market value, giving him a general idea of how much he could expect to get in Taiwan for a secondhand Grotrian, obtainable here for eighteen thousand dollars?

Once we were in operation, who but I could be entrusted with tuning the old pianos to fulfill every client's dream?

Emily came up during our dinner now and then, as if she had been sitting silently at our table.

Lin *san* told me that he and Emily had visited London, Paris, and Vienna but had not managed to produce memories of New York. He'd mentioned a trip to New York several times, but she hadn't wanted to come, saying there would be time enough and that she wanted to see Europe first. Having studied in the United States, she didn't feel an urgent need to come back for a visit.

A man who called himself a savvy businessman could not possibly fail to sense something unusual in her reaction. How could he not tell it had just been an excuse?

I knew we could continue to work together only so long as my sympathy for him went unnoticed.

Maybe it was just as he believed, that every relationship is built on a balanced foundation of supply and demand. What did I have to lose if I was treated as a piece of driftwood amid his loss and sense of emptiness following the death of his wife?

Then, for reasons beyond me, the image of the pianist and his French lover flashed through my mind.

I was convinced that they must have dined here often when they were at the height of their careers.

Before my hopes for the four-hand duet were dashed, I might have fantasized about the pianist taking me to cities where he would perform.

Maybe it wasn't fantasy; he might have instilled that hope without meaning to. It is cruel and dangerous to make that sort of promise to a seventeen-year-old.

What if—yet another what-if—he'd confronted me when he saw his cherished Steinway badly scratched? What if I'd had the courage to confess what I'd done? And might it be, in fact, that I never gave him the chance to fulfill his promise?

None of this mattered now, however.

I turned back from surveying the red interior of the restaurant and expressed gratitude that even I found awkward to express.

"Thank you for the trip, Mr. Lin."

Maybe my balanced supply-and-demand relationship with a man who looked more like a musician than I did was built on forgetting.

He would eventually have to forget Emily, who had never really loved him, while I had finally made it to the pianist's city.

8

Our fifth day in New York.

We had nothing planned, because he had to go to Philadelphia to meet his ex-wife and son for a family lunch.

If what he'd said was true about these visits giving him an ulcer, I imagined he would be in a funk when he returned to New York in the evening. So, before we left the hotel for our respective activity, I made a point of suggesting that I check the box office at Lincoln Center. Maybe there'd be tickets for that night's concert, which I hoped would help with his mood. I was surprised to hear him reply:

"How about a Broadway musical? It's been a long time since I've seen one."

I was relieved by his suggestion.

As a matter of fact, I didn't really want to go to a concert, especially not at Alice Tully Hall, where the pianist had left such an important imprint of his life.

After buying the tickets, I spent the rest of the day strolling aimlessly. By the time the day ended, I'd seen thirteen violinists playing on sidewalks, subway platforms, or parks of various sizes, hoping for tips from passersby.

I was mildly dizzy, but that might have been caused by the dropping temperature. Dusk descended at four in the afternoon, as cold winds blew in from the waters surrounding Manhattan, like knives carving me up to make a new body. I no longer had a form whose outlines had been blurred by years of soaking in high humidity.

Each breath was more like inhaling shards of ice into my lungs, which led to the illusion that my body had regained the sharp edges of its younger self.

The younger days. I remembered.

Back then, there were no seasonal divisions. Summer was so long it was stifling, and westerly winds were the only poetic images. I survived by imagining a snowfall.

With the sun gone, the temperature dropped to near zero. I'd never been so close to an imminent snowfall.

I'd made a special trip home before leaving for New York. Mother now lived alone in a public housing unit by the old military airport, which Father had bought with money saved from twenty years of selling dumplings.

Luckily, except for a hearing problem, she could still

manage on her own. Being the youngest child, with two older brothers and two older sisters, I'd drifted all these years, without doing much for the family. As I sat in the living room with Mother, watching a Korean soap opera and explaining the plot to her, I was pained by the thought that she would have to stare blankly at the scenes on the TV screen if no one was around to help her.

I never told her much about my personal life, let alone something that hadn't even taken shape. Would the plan of trading secondhand pianos really come to fruition? My current job as a tuner was part-time work, just enough to support myself. When would I be able to share the responsibility of caring for Mother?

During a commercial break, Mother recalled a Ms. Chiu, who had phoned and asked me to contact her.

Ms. Chiu, now sixty, had just retired from her college teaching job. Her daughter, who lived in Canada, had arranged an immigration visa, and she'd be leaving as early as the end of the month.

I could hardly be considered her best student, and yet she remembered me enough to want to see me. I couldn't say how that made me feel, grateful or somewhat reluctant. The gentle, loving, pretty young woman with graceful airs in my childhood memory was wearing her hair short and had turned into a matronly woman.

She'd always worked hard. While teaching primary

school, she'd taken enough classes to become a high school teacher. Then she'd gone abroad to earn a master's degree, which had earned her an instructorship at an educational junior college. She'd then taken an unpaid leave to earn a doctorate in music education overseas, during which time she'd met her future husband, who was studying information management. Later, the junior college had expanded into a regular four-year college and then into a full-blown university. Eventually, she'd become a college professor, even serving as dean of academic affairs for several years.

After a lifetime of tireless, diligent work, the retirement was well-earned. I should have been happy for her. Fortunately, nothing had developed between her and the pianist, whom she'd clearly adored.

But I simply could not make the connection between the Ms. Chiu before me and the woman from years earlier. An unspeakable sadness overtook me. I wanted to ask her what else, besides the pianist and me, both of whom had disappointed her, had cropped up to push her youthful dream further and further away.

"I think of you often."

She said as she put on her reading glasses and retrieved a manila envelope from under the tea table, "I found this as I was packing. Look."

Inside was a pile of certificates and awards I'd earned at competitions.

"You told me you couldn't take them home to show

your father and asked me to keep them for you. I'd forgotten all about them, but here they are."

Maybe she'd forgotten all about her dreams too.

Maybe she wanted to see me because she needed someone, another one who had given up, to mark the end, to make herself feel better.

"This is my husband."

"How do you do, sir?"

I gave a hurried bow to the figure walking in. He had a towel around his neck and a canteen over his shoulder. He'd been mountain climbing or hiking.

He was short and stocky. Even in retirement he wore a calm, determined look, as if he'd made up his mind to live out his old age in a dignified manner. With a smile, he greeted me before disappearing from the living room. Obviously, they had a tacit agreement to keep their social circles separate. "Neat and tidy." I finally found the words to describe the feeling I had from the moment I walked into her house.

Once we stopped talking about music, our meeting was like any old friends catching up. I was approaching middle age. For a brief moment, I thought I would tear up without warning, especially when she changed the subject and asked why I was still single. "Haven't you met anyone suitable?"

Ms. Chiu of thirty years before would have never asked a question like that. But I didn't feel like arguing with the

Ms. Chiu before me. What had she meant by "suitable"? It wasn't even a good word to describe the pairing of a piano and a musician, but when used for two people, it turned into a self-evident, conventional guideline. Was I the only who didn't know what the word meant?

Had she known her husband was the "suitable" person when she met him thirty years ago? If their relationship smoothed out over half a lifetime of effort, then it had nothing to do with "suitability" and everything to do with accepting one's lot.

"I'm going to New York next week," I mentioned, as if in passing, when I got up to leave.

She looked momentarily lost, as if she'd never heard of the place, but quickly put on a smile, like a teacher sending off graduates, an expression that betrayed lifelessness while insisting upon a rosy outlook on life.

"Oh, really? Have fun. There's so much to see in New York."

I'd expected her to say more.

It dawned on me that, to her, the pianist belonged to a meaningless past.

Lin *san* raced to the theater fifteen minutes before the curtain rose that evening. He glanced at the people waiting outside but failed to spot me right off.

"New cap?"

"Yeah. I was at St. Mark's in East Village this afternoon

and saw this beret. I'm fond of burgundy, so I tossed my beat-up cap."

He checked me out, saying it looked good on me. Before I had a chance to ask about lunch with the family, he wanted to know what I'd done all day. So, I opened my backpack and took out a plastic bag containing a dozen or more refrigerator magnets.

I'd collected them at all the souvenir shops, flea markets, and secondhand stores along the way.

"All musical instruments," I said. "Saxophone, guitar, piano, trumpet, violin, cello, and on and on. All for you."

Lights flashed inside signaling that the show was about to start. He reached into the bag, grabbed one, and put it in his pocket.

9

T IMBRE.

When a piano key is pressed, our acoustic nerve receives the timbre's three parts.

The first can be called the basic note, *wang-wang*. The second, sounding like *chiang-chiang*, defines the force and clarity of a musical note.

The third, with the addition of expression in the sound, a bit like shades of light, is regulated by *sz-sz*. Proportional adjustment among the three sounds, *wang-wang*, *chiang-chiang*, and *sz-sz*, creates the timbre our ears detect.

It differs from temperament or pitch, which can be approximated through mathematic calculation, even though we cannot achieve 100 percent accuracy. Timbre is purely a subjective preference, just as the way one is naturally predisposed to like certain types of people. We can't explain whether it's something predestined or the workings of our brain cells, though usually we tend to believe it is a kind of instinct.

To the average ear, a sonorous and rich tone is beautiful, but the layers of timbre are more than that. Some sonorous notes are sharp, like cut diamonds, while others are as dulcet as pearls. Is a rich timbre bright, like a ray of the sun, or lyrical, like murmuring water?

How do we understand the timbre demanded by a musician? A sound color might as well not exist if it cannot be described by vivid, accurate words. It's a challenge that needs to be overcome by two people who must have a similar understanding of the words.

A tuner must be prepared for the self-professed specialists, clients who believe they are a cut above, when they say, "A bit somber, somewhat bleak and yet warm, expansive but subtle."

A tuner has to force himself to keep from laughing out loud.

Melody can be written down; an emotional display that echoes segments of a performance can be imitated. Timbre alone can never fall into a pattern, for no matter how exquisite it may be, it is always ephemeral.

It goes without saying that repeated strikes over time

will change the timbre, but most people would rather stay with what comes first, joy that is akin to love at first sight.

What exactly do those people want to hold on to?

No matter how creative the client's abstract descriptions may be, there is little a tuner can do.

Tuning mainly involves adjusting the hardness of the hammer by pricking the felt with needles, even soaking it in a chemical solution, in order to create varying but distinct strikes when it comes into contact with the string, either strengthening or lengthening the ratio between *wang-wang, chiang-chiang,* or *sz-sz.* That's all.

Would piano owners still be so adamant in their demands if they understood that, to satisfy their ears, the hammers must be heavily damaged? Would a so-called perfect lover fashioned by cosmetic surgery possess unique qualities?

Is it possible that a musician's subjective search for a particular sound color is based on a memory of hearing it somewhere and not from a genuine internal vibration? As time goes by, the memory might possibly become inaccurate or twisted, thus transformed into a kind of aural hallucination.

If we could find a primitive tribe free of all contact with the outside world and let the people hear their very first piano piece, what sort of desire and image would it call to their minds?

And how would they use words to describe the sounds they heard?

My ears are superb in distinguishing musical temperament; I have an exceptional memory; and I can discriminate between minute differences in sound colors. But, paradoxically, I've never had a personal timbre preference.

To someone who could never own a piano, being picky about a piano's sound color amounts to self-deception.

Maybe that was why I believed I was better suited to be a tuner than a pianist or a piano teacher. I could always stay aloof from a pianist's stubborn insistence on a perfection of timbre.

Tuning work let me maintain minimal contact with the outside world. I'd thought it was a blessing to be trusted and depended on.

But being trusted is not the same as being complicit.

Initially attracted to Emily's contradictions and complexity, I thought I was finally able to hear a timbre that was different from all others.

Surprisingly, Emily did not cancel my tuning service immediately after the incident. So I continued tirelessly to produce a variety of sound colors for her to choose from but wound up making it even harder for her to judge. In the end, she actually asked me, "So what do you think?"

"The best solution now is to replace all the hammer felts," I said. "Then learn to accept what they produce. You'll ruin the piano if you keep going like this."

Her geniality and the subsequent helplessness she displayed only intensified my awareness of our inequality. Understanding that I was below her, she didn't even bother to make an introduction when the man showed up again. I wondered if I'd stuck around not because of her occasional display of tenderness, but out of a desire to see how she'd been misused by a younger man.

She invariably reminded me of the Steinway I'd savagely scratched with a screw many years before.

My hopeless descent had nothing to do with sex or love; it was self-loathing.

By putting on a pitiful, humiliated look in her presence, I somehow gained an advantage, for despite her contempt for and fear of me, she had to treat me as her sole ally. If not for the sudden cancer diagnosis, I was convinced that, in the end, the ponytailed man would have had to treat me with respect and would have regretted not practicing self-restraint around me.

When I showed up again a year later, I reached out and hit a key on her Steinway to produce a note that was slightly off, muted, sad but kind. The sound color stunned me, as if someone were whispering in my ear, "Please don't go."

*

Who was imprisoned in that piano?

New York's nightlife, it turned out, doesn't take place on the famous avenues.

When we reached the Hudson River, a hinterland of sorts, the vista changed to reveal a street with brightly lit restaurants.

Lin *san*, who had missed out on dinner because of the musical, perked up at the sight, his weariness gone. Over the week we spent in New York, he often chose to eat at restaurants he'd visited before.

It could be a cafeteria-style burger joint or a small Greek place in an old building deep down a side street. When the musical ended at ten that night, he was in high spirits as he dragged me along to seek out an Italian family-run restaurant with a fifty-year history.

"You find authentic flavors only in an old place like this, with red and white plastic checkered tablecloths and an old grandma taking money behind the counter," he said.

After we sat down and placed our order, I finally had a chance to ask about his trip to Philly. He sighed and said his son's stepfather, his ex-wife's current husband, was diagnosed with lung cancer and quit his job to undergo treatment.

"It's absurd, don't you think? We both thought we'd never make the same mistake the second time, but in the end, we're, well, we're in the same boat."

Ours was the only quiet table in the crowded restaurant. English felt, to me at least, like the perfect background language. It sounded like stage plays being rehearsed at tables, the diners practicing familiar dialogue and roles.

Recalling how Lin *san* had taken a magnet from my bag of souvenirs just before the show, I took the bag out of my backpack, laid it on the table, and repeated my offer.

"Guess which piece I took?" He reached into his pocket. "No taking stock of what's left allowed. Gut feeling."

Looking at a balled fist with the answer inside, I felt a sudden melancholy. Shaking my head, I told myself maybe I never wanted to know.

When he saw no response from me, he laughed lightly and opened his fist. A trumpet. "I'm surprised you would think of giving me something like this."

On his first trip to New York to expand his market, he'd stayed in a short-term sublet he'd found in the classified ads. He recalled that the refrigerator door was covered with these little things, something he'd never seen before. In fact, he even studied them to see if there might be a market for them in Taiwan.

"I took a detour to see that apartment and almost didn't make it to the show on time." He fiddled with the trinket. "I was there only for a month, but I can still recall its interior."

"Did you meet the renters? What were they like?" His recollection piqued my interest. "When was that?"

"Almost thirty years ago now. I was just starting out, and hotels were too expensive. Someone told me this was the way to save money. The renter was a Japanese overseas student who was going home for summer break and didn't want to pay rent while he was away. A really nice kid, even sent a postcard from Japan to ask me if everything was okay."

He paused pensively before looking from his palm to my face.

"Sublets are popular in America, but to me it's odd how people can trust a complete stranger to move into their place, sleep in their bed, and use their stuff. It's like living in somebody's house, taking that person's place."

His emotional reflection seemed to come out of nowhere, and I didn't know how to respond. If someone sitting in a corner hadn't caught my eye at that moment, I might have noticed that the trip to Philly had unsettled Lin *san*.

What happened next can only be described as too sudden for me to react.

The man sitting behind Lin facing my way locked eyes with me, but only for a second. His gaze moved on. He had no idea who I was.

That didn't startle me, though I hadn't expected Manhattan to be so small.

He was wearing a mustard green jacket and a purple scarf that day, a flashy outfit I'd thought was only found on down-and-out performers. But what caught my attention were his single-fold eyes and ponytail. As he was walking toward the cash register, he stopped at our table and called out:

"Douglas!"

Then he came up, gave Lin a hug, and said sorrowfully, a couple of times, "I'm so sorry."

I froze, just for a moment, before realizing that he wasn't apologizing for his transgression. He was expressing condolences over Emily's death.

So, Lin had an English name, Douglas.

The man chatted with Lin *san*, oblivious to my presence, as I, the person who knew everything, coolly watched his performance.

Their interaction told me they hadn't seen each other for a very long time. The memorial service for Emily had been six months before. He hadn't shown, and yet he was shamelessly pretending to be sad. I felt heat roar up from my chest to my head. Lin *san*, who had been sentimentally nostalgic just minutes earlier, put on a smiley face and asked the man to join us while making the introductions,

"This was Emily's student, Jiawei—I should be calling you Gary, shouldn't I? I certainly never expected to see you here. You haven't been back to Taiwan for some time, have you?" He turned to me. "You probably didn't know that Emily taught middle school for a few years. Jiawei is very talented. He came to America for high school and graduated from Julliard, majoring in piano. Did I get that right?"

Was it because of the beret, or was he pretending he didn't know me? No, it had to be my humble, common appearance that made Ponytail lose interest in me after an expressionless nod.

A question flashed through my mind too fast for me to mull it over. It was confusing and disorienting to see the two men chatting so amicably there in front of me.

Emily never mentioned that he'd been her middle-school student.

If it hadn't been an excuse she made up for Lin *san's* sake, then when had their relationship started? When they met again after she came to the United States? Or had she picked Boston University so they could continue their clandestine affair on the East Coast?

Lin *san* was at a loss for words when it came to introducing me to Ponytail, either because he forgot my name or because he didn't want to tell Ponytail why he and I were in New York.

Over the past three months or so, it had been just the two of us, making it natural to address each other as "you." When we communicated through technology, my account handle was "piano man." To Lin *san*, I really was a man with no name.

The future of the music studio was uncertain. If he didn't

want to say too much, especially to Emily's former student, he must have found it difficult to introduce someone like me, with no professional title or impressive degree.

"This is my partner."

After a brief silence, Lin *san* shifted his gaze to my face, as if what he'd just uttered was an exam question with no solution.

"Partner? You mean business partner, don't you?"

I wondered why Ponytail insisted upon speaking English. I knew for a fact that he spoke fluent Mandarin. When he heard the term Lin *san* used, a mocking smile betrayed itself over the unfortunate use of that word, as if teasing him for not knowing that in New York, partner referred to homosexual couples.

"Ah, well if you're business partners, you must have important things to talk about, so I'll say good-bye."

Ponytail hadn't planned to hang around, nor did he care who I was. So, after a bit of small talk, he quick-stepped away, though it felt to me more like bolting.

How could Lin *san* not know the many uses of the word partner? Even *I* learned that in my high school English class. Not exclusively used for business or homosexual couples, it originally meant just that, a partner, like in tennis or bridge.

My irritation and bewilderment caused by the interruption lingered. I was particularly outraged that the guy had actually used a teasing, flighty tone to make a totally ill-advised joke about us. There was no way Lin *san* and I looked like a couple.

"That Gary, he didn't seem like a very likable guy. Look at his outfit and what he said about partners. He must be gay."

"He's not." Lin *san* picked up his knife and fork calmly to go after the veal cutlet on his plate. "Got something against gays? Where did that come from?"

His smile was gone, and I could not control my mouth. I don't know why, but at that moment I was seized by the desire to piss him off. My anger was shifting in a different direction without my knowing it. I felt more humiliated by the smile on Lin *san*'s face just now than by the way Ponytail had dismissed me.

"I could tell with one look that he's a poser. Why be so nice to someone that phony? Speaking English the whole time. He speaks Mandarin. So what if he's gay? Why did he have to act like a big shot?"

"Oh, how do you know he speaks Mandarin?"

"Didn't you say he left for high school in America?" I hadn't expected him to listen to my rant so carefully. "And why change the subject?"

"His English is probably better than his Chinese now."

"And you know that how? The guy—"

"Why are you so interested in him?"

He'd finally run out of patience. "I can tell you I know

perfectly well that he's not gay. I also know he likes older women."

That shut me up.

As if a hammer had thumped me on the forehead, I looked at him dumbly, unable to react. Was that a joke to end the conversation? Or was it a warning?

Devoid of anger or disdain, he wore a look that said, Don't you believe me?

Over the next few seconds, we sat there staring at each other wordlessly, I kept hearing a jumble of discordant, sharp notes, *chiang-chiang-chiang, chiang-chiang-chiang,* like a toddler banging away on a toy piano in an invisible corner, where he could keep at it until the thing fell apart.

Maybe Emily had revealed to her lover something about her marriage, something she could not share with anyone else.

If Ponytail's mockery wasn't a complete shot in the dark, that is.

I'd thought I held in my hand the secret of their marriage, but it was possible they had no secrets. Providing each other with cover through marriage is not worth making a fuss over.

I almost wondered if this was a prank pulled by Emily from another dimension. The coincidence was simply too hard to accept, running into Ponytail in a city of several million.

*

God used music to trick souls into physical bodies, the pianist had said.

Souls had been equal, while flesh wasn't. Therefore, in the human world equality can be achieved only through art.

His added interpretation to the story suddenly occurred to me. Did he still believe in it when he died?

The ears were satisfied by music, but not the other sensory organs. If there weren't flesh, what kind of world would the pianist, Emily, Lin *san*, Ms. Chiu, and I be living in? Would our encounters tell different stories?

I finally understood the agony the pianist had suffered back then. He had conquered the piano and the ears of music fans but had failed to tame his body. Flesh can be satisfied only through cruel, savage measures.

I looked away, beset by regret over my loss of self-control. Jumping to my feet, I said I was going to the bathroom. In fact, I stood outside the toilet, watching diners go in and out while trying to regain my composure.

Would the silhouette that remained in the seat facing an empty chair across the table be my future portrait?

Peeking out through the cheap plastic flower trellis, I saw him pick up the bag of souvenirs and toss in the one he'd held earlier. Then he folded the bag and placed it on the empty chair next to him under his coat.

How could a man like him, who had everything, be so easily moved by inexpensive gifts? His action did not make me feel better, actually mortified me. I had to fight the urge to go out there, snatch the bag back, and throw everything in it away.

Wouldn't the souls that had been tricked into entering physical bodies think of exchanging their unimportant and fragile shells?

If Lin *san's* soul were paired with the pianist's body, or my soul were to enter a shell with blond hair and blue eyes, would there then be no regrets?

I was barely in my seat when he said he wanted to talk about the next day's itinerary, our last stop, a piano warehouse in the Bronx.

He seemed as calm as when we'd walked into the restaurant, as if nothing had happened. I asked if he really believed that the plan to repurpose the music studio would work. If not, it made no sense to go out there. As if he hadn't been listening, he simply said that we should head back to the hotel for an early start the next day.

Left with no choice, I nodded and forced a smile.

After he paid, we walked to the door, where I was greeted by a complete change of scenery. "Oh, my God!" I blurted out.

He looked confused until he saw me staring at the sky beyond the glass door. An understanding smile broke out. "First snowfall?"

Snowflakes weren't drifting slowly down the way I'd seen in cartoons as a child. They were actually swirling madly in gusty wind among the high-rises.

Streetlights shone on them, tiny dots of black and patches of white falling to the ground, like splintered black and white piano keys.

Did a snowflake know it would become snow before it fell from the sky?

Staring transfixed into the sky, I fantasized twirling and flying with the snowflakes high above Manhattan.

Did it ever think it could be a raindrop or a hailstone? Or did it dream of turning into sleet or the backdrop for a rainbow?

Until one day, when it spread its wings to greet the ground, it realized it had turned into a snowflake?

An unfamiliar city with unfamiliar snow.

Two men walked side by side in the swirling snow. The sounds of their footsteps on streets dusted with snow were uneven, discordant, like an ensemble piano piece needing no strings. We took our time returning to the hotel, where the staff was busy salting the sidewalk and shoveling the snow, quickly restoring the entrance to its former spotless state.

My ears might have been ringing from the excitement, but more likely, the falling snow wasn't entirely silent.

I thought I heard faint low notes hanging in the air, like vibrations from the throats of chanting monks.

Before walking in, I looked up again to see that the blanketing snow had created a different canvas in the sky, like a starry night. A pair of hands reaching out to thump the snow off my coat caught me unawares.

Tomorrow at eight in the lobby?

I nodded.

When we reached our facing rooms, before taking out my key card, I copied the common good-night scenes on the city's street corners by giving him a hasty hug.

10

On the stage, Richter slowly rose to face the audience and, bent slightly at the waist, nodded. The concert hall was hushed.

No one dared ruining such a solemn yet stirring moment.

Not someone who normally gave interviews, he made a rare exception in his later years by agreeing to a documentary proposed by French director Bruno Monsaingeon. It was called *Richter: The Enigma*, shown the year after Richter's death, enabling tens of millions of his fans to see a more authentic maestro behind the stage.

He was his own world, private and brilliant. In Monsaingeon's words, Richter played without flair but with total freedom.

But was that true? Didn't the title of the film indicate

that Richter was an enigmatic person, whom no one could really know? When I first located the film on YouTube, I almost said, "What do you think?"

Too bad the pianist died too soon to see the film.

I could not help imagining how he would react if he were watching it with me. When he saw the aging maestro, who wished to leave a record behind, as if aware of his mortality, would he be pleased not to have to explain himself in the face of his inevitable physical deterioration?

Especially when it got to the part where Richter talked about his lifelong companion, Nina Dorliak, the singer.

Their romance had not started out with a passion-filled courtship or love at first sight. The maestro said he remembered with great clarity the first time he heard her sing; that was followed by a jump cut to show a haggard, aging Nina.

"He came to see me one day and asked if I wanted to give a concert with him," she said. "He was quite well known by then, so I said, 'Is it going to be part piano recital and part solo singing?' I was surprised to hear his offer to 'accompany me.'"

Just like that, a shining star in music was her accompanist. Recalling it forty years later, Nina still could not hide her joy at being so favored.

The soundtrack then returns to Richter: "In 1946 I moved in with her. Before that, I did not have a place of my own. I lived in government housing I shared with another family."

A perfect partnership, lifelong companions. Nina died only months after Richter. They were together almost till their last days but were never formally married, as if living together to improve their quality of life was the natural thing to do.

Everyone said they formed a spiritual union and that everything beyond that was left to individual interpretation.

Then comes the part of the documentary dealing with choosing a piano.

Surprisingly, his normally weak, lethargic voice turns unusually passionate: "I don't know how to choose a piano. I never did know. When I went to America, they told me to pick one out of a dozen. That ruined my performance.

"Picking out a piano is detrimental to a musician, it is like choosing one's fate; the more you try, the worse it gets.

"That should be the job of a tuner. It's like St. Peter, whose piety let him walk on water. Without faith, he'd have sunk. I sometimes played exceptionally well on a terrible piano."

What confidence! How headstrong!

But obviously, the interviewer detected a contradiction. It wasn't that Richter wouldn't choose a piano; he simply did not know how. The interviewer persisted:

"What do you look for in a piano?"

Like a suspect under interrogation, he inadvertently revealed the truth:

"I've never found the one I want." He sounded so helpless, as if talking about something other than pianos, and was prepared to bare the emptiness in his soul from never obtaining what he wanted.

Then the maestro regains his calm and adds unhurriedly: "Sound color is the key. Yamaha pianos have what I look for—pianissimo. The most affecting color isn't the most powerful, but it has the subtlest, the softest note."

Indeed, he always took a Yamaha piano along when he toured in his later years, as if that were the only way to eliminate his fear of having to choose one. And that was why, even given his aversion to flying overseas for concerts, he made eight trips to Japan.

One can see the contradiction in his confession by looking more carefully. When was the last time he'd shown an indifference to pianos, any of which, as he claimed, he could play even if it were terrible?

Could it be that his confidence was a put-on? Early on, he had a tuner he trusted pick a piano for him. Later, he was forced to play a Yamaha because his tuner had left him.

Hey, didn't you once say you could go on stage only with your Austrian tuner present? I shouted to the imagined pianist beside me.

A decision had to be made between "I've never found the one I want," and "I don't know how to choose a piano. I never did know."

Aren't all the people in the world just like the myriad types of pianos, in a way—they all dazzle the eye.

So, what do you think? Did Richter find Nina among a crowd or did she choose him?

I got out of bed without turning on the light and walked in the dark to open the window curtain. The snow was still coming down hard, and I decided not to close the curtain, turning the snow framed by the window into a painting. I began to feel dizzy after staring at the snow scene too long; the endlessly swirling snowflakes turned into a mighty army that could crash into a window and disintegrate with no regrets.

Snow isn't always light and airy; it can be quite powerful, I found.

When I think about it, I realize that this was my most unforgettable image of New York. Everything else was adulterated with too many preconceptions from what I'd heard elsewhere, as well as from my own imagination.

I had a sleepless night. What Ponytail had said and done at the restaurant kept replaying in my head, in bits and pieces, and there seemed to be other fragmentary entanglements as well. Mostly, the insomnia was caused by the reappearance of a specter.

Yes, there is no better word than specter.

The previous night should have been the moment he and I could have once more talked freely over drinks. I missed the small pub we'd gone to in Taipei. Since becoming partners, we rarely talked about anything other than business.

After revisiting the encounter in my head, I consoled myself that running into Ponytail had not been a total disaster.

His appearance released the tension over some concerns. I no longer had to keep Emily's secret or feel like Lin *san*'s factotum. I could even say to Emily, "You can go now. Take care. If only you could see what I've done for him these past few days . . ."

After straining to put Ponytail out of my mind, I began to sense that my memory of Emily was crumbling, becoming distorted. I went back to bed, turned on my laptop, and put on my Bluetooth headphones. Listening to Rachmaninoff for the first time in a while, I browsed websites about piano sales. A mail notification window popped up. It was a message from Ms. Chiu.

My dear child,
I've almost finished packing and we'll be leaving Taiwan in two days.

I was so pleased to see you the other day.

Actually, I called and left messages, but
your mother might have forgotten to tell
you. I'm relieved I was able to get back in
touch with you before leaving.

When I saw her address me as "child," I had to laugh,
but at the same time it gave me a wistful feeling.

Calculating the time difference, I imagined her sitting
in her study in the afternoon, with her reading glasses on,
slowly pecking out these words. The parting sorrow I'd
suppressed when bidding her farewell finally surfaced. I'd
been tugged this way and that by too many emotions, and
I could only read on with feelings of guilt.

After not seeing one another for more than
twenty years, we'd both changed a lot. I'm
happy to know you haven't given up on
the piano. You were in second grade when
I forced you to stay after school to play.
Remember?

Thinking back, I realize I was just a young
teacher fresh out of a music department.
If it were now, I might have different ideas
about how to teach a musical prodigy. So
many years have gone by, but I still feel
remorse and worry about what I did. I was

so inexperienced I wonder if I did the right
thing, or if I had a negative influence on you.

Some things are hard to say face-to-face,
so I'm taking the trouble to write this letter.
As someone in her twenties, I was envious
and somewhat jealous of your natural gifts
and talent. I was proud, however, to be
your first teacher. I was vaguely aware at
the time that I was getting further away
from being a concert pianist. But my dream
was reignited after I met you, except, at
such a young age, I didn't truly understand
the meaning of dreams.

Ms. Chiu, graceful, with long hair and a soft voice,
came toward me from the other end of time. No, it wasn't
you, I mumbled to myself repeatedly. It wasn't you who
hurt me, not you.

Pulling the earbuds off, I looked over at the swirling
snow outside and took a deep breath.

In recent years I've been telling my students
that dreams aren't meant to be pursued,
nor to be owned or conquered. They should
be like your conscience, a sincere melody in
your heart, not something external.

Claiming they're chasing after or building
a dream, many young people make plan
after plan, some of which work out, some
don't. The so-called dreams turn into mere
records of real life.

Please don't think I'm lecturing you. I'm no
longer qualified to be your music teacher,
and I'm sure you'll achieve more than I
ever did. I just want to share what I've
experienced and learned over the past two
decades, is that all right?

Now that I've come to this point, I might
as well share with you something even my
husband doesn't know. LOL

Tears were already welling up in my eyes, but I laughed
out loud over the surprise. I was right, wasn't I? Every marriage has its secrets, and not even an upright person with a
sunny personality, like Ms. Chiu, can be an exception.

I went abroad to study the second time
when I turned thirty, a cinch to earn a PhD
in music education, but no one knew that
for a while I felt terribly lost. Loneliness is
inevitable when you're alone in a foreign

country, and I fell head over heels for a
Hispanic man who had dreams of being an
actor. In the summer of 1992, we decided
to move to New York, for at the time it
occurred to me that that was my dream,
spending the rest of my life with someone I
loved. I'd waited so many years and finally
here he was. I was willing to give up my
doctoral studies for him.

I wasn't as uptight as you thought. There
was actually a moment when I had the
courage to seek love.

Ha! Nice going! I just had to slap my thigh, but then a
hint of dolefulness overtook me, freezing the smile at the
corners of my mouth. Who could have known that even
Ms. Chiu had experienced an unforgettable romance?

We lived in New York for six months. I gave
piano lessons in the Chinese community in
the daytime and played at small bars in the
Village at night. To earn tips from customers
with requests, I learned many Broadway
tunes I'd never heard of. My boyfriend
continued to audition, all with the same
result, but he didn't give up. Like so many

aspiring actors in the city, he waited tables at a restaurant while waiting for his chance.

At first it all felt so new and joyful. From a very young age, I'd been a good student with no behavioral issues. I didn't become a famous concert pianist, but becoming a college professor ought to be enough to demonstrate my potential. I thought I was living for myself and no longer cared about mundane matters. But six months went by, and we started fighting over money, and I realized that you still have to worry about daily necessities, even when your dream is fulfilled.

Do you remember Joseph, the pianist I wanted you to study with? I saw him in New York and learned that he was seriously ill. One night a few months before he passed away, he and I were listening to the album he'd recorded during the golden days of his musical career, when he exclaimed, "Where do you think your home is?"

I was stumped for an answer. At that moment I realized I was nostalgic for the

days when I'd practiced the most difficult
classical pieces. As I walked down brightly
lit Broadway and looked at all the people
who had come here to chase their dreams,
I'd learned that life isn't black or white, and
that what we call dreams can only occur at
the right time and place for the right people.

A real dream is a force to prop you up when
you're helpless and lost, which I felt most
keenly after Joseph's death.

I know I'm rambling, but I just want to tell
you, I've never regretted the detour I took
in New York, nor do I rue my lack of better
gifts. I chose family and opted to return to
Taiwan, decisions that will not likely help
me advance further along but best fit the
melody in my heart.

I hope you didn't mind my asking you about
finding someone suitable. I wasn't prying.
I watched you grow up, and I could see
some things more clearly than you could.
I thought you might be having romance
issues, for you looked distracted that day

at my house. I wasn't afraid all those years ago, and I hope you too can let yourself go. Don't be afraid. You only live once. You are someone with a dream, and I'm sure it will happen for you at the right moment to help you recover the main theme of your life.

Tuning pianos is challenging work, and you're just starting out, so it may not bring in a steady income.

I'll help you by recommending clients. I've talked to the music hall director at the university about the possibility of hiring you as the "resident tuner" to maintain the two grand pianos reserved for concerts.

Ah, I should say three pianos. I forgot about the Steinway that is seldom used because of the cosmetic damage. Joseph donated it to our school just before his death. At the time he—

I couldn't read any more. The air from the heater was so dry I had trouble breathing.

I opened the window, and immediately the snow, like a

mad army, rushed in on icy cold air. Caught between arctic winter and sweltering summer, I stood by the window in a daze.

So many years later, on a night when real snow fell on me . . .

Who released the specter in that piano, so it could travel around the world to find me?

•

11

THE SNOW CONTINUED into the following morning. Having a sudden change of heart, Lin *san* decided not to take the train but to rent a car to drive to the Bronx. It was quiet in the car, except for a cough he'd developed.

"I didn't sleep well. Got a cold, I think," he said.

After the surprise encounter, I'd tossed and turned, my mind occupied with all sorts of thoughts, unable to sleep, but I wasn't the only one, obviously.

Had Emily really blown past him and me like a gust of wind? With her no longer as an invisible bridge between us, he and I silently watched the windshield wipers clear the snow, as if waiting for a computer to restart.

Until he abruptly spoke up.

"Can you go back on your own the day after tomorrow? I want to spend some time here."

I tried to suppress my surprise, though I couldn't help feeling degraded by his offhanded notification. Were all rich people willful and unpredictable?

"My son. I told you he's going to college next year, didn't I? The man is seriously ill, and my ex-wife says it doesn't look good, maybe six months, maybe not even that—"

The stifling silence in that tiny space along the way had prepared me for what was coming, actually. He might not be only asking me to return alone, for I sensed he was about to make some kind of announcement.

"Life will be tough for the mother and son from now on. What worries me most is my son. We won't have much time together after he leaves for college. As a father, I . . . ai, I won't bore you, but, if I'm honest with myself, I haven't been much of a father."

The wipers diligently cleared the snow off the windshield. When he paused, the only sound was a rhythmic scraping, like a phonograph needle skipping over a vinyl. He was worried about his son, about that other family losing their support. All very reasonable and fair. So why did he feel he had to explain it to me?

"What's your plan for the future? What if we're to halt our project for now—"

Voilà! Sure enough. There. Told you.

A tactful tone brimming with concern while explaining a difficult situation to the person he'd soon fire. He'd called me his partner, though we had yet to establish a formal relationship of employer and employee, but he really didn't need to sound so careful and apologetic, despite our undefined differences in status.

"If you've made up your mind, why are we making this trip?" I couldn't hold back.

"It will just be halted for now. I need a year to make it up to my son, that's why I want to talk to you. I'd like to know what you'll be doing during this time."

Had he lost sleep over this? Or, after Ponytail's veiled mockery, had he finally opened his eyes to see who I really was, not someone he wanted around.

"If you think it'll work, I don't mind if you go it alone. I wrote down the pianos we talked about, and I can place the order anytime. But I'll understand if you think we should stop now—to be honest, I've been wondering what's on your mind—are you doing this just to help me out? Do you really want to go into this business, or—"

Or what? I almost said, but lacked the courage to go on, for I was afraid he'd say we were deceiving ourselves with our earlier persistence.

What kind of interpersonal relationship would remain once the word "partner" was stripped of gender, sexuality, and money?

Why me? How could it ever have been me? Wouldn't he want a partner who was more presentable, more sophisticated?

He turned the wheel, eased the car to the side, and turned off the engine.

"I find you really confusing lately. Are you still the same person I met a while back? I thought you were coolheaded and steady, but what was going on at the restaurant last night?"

I sensed his displeasure, but looked straight ahead, my lips pressed tight.

"But that has nothing to do with what we're talking about. I just want to remind you that, once we become partners, you'll have to take charge. It will be more than just tuning the pianos. Are you aware of that? That's why I said you can start working when you get back to Taipei or you can wait until I take care of my son here. If you feel you're not up to it, that's OK. The music studio will be shut down no matter what, and I can always come up with something."

He had pushed me step by step to this spot, and now he was saying I was the problem. Obviously, he had forgotten how disconsolate he'd been three months earlier, what with the piano making noise at midnight, and feeling abandoned by his friends. I couldn't have conjured those up, could I? He'd revealed all this to me in the little pub.

What if I were to stay? With the two of us remaining in New York, would that mean freedom for both of us?

But now that we'd come to this, I'd humiliate myself if I made any more suggestions.

I should have breathed a sigh of relief, for I'd finally found a way out; instead, I was disconcerted, as if a jumble of piano keys were banging away in my head. Could it be that once again I'd been overeager in my one-sided, wishful thinking? I helped others tune and adjust their instruments, and yet I'd ended up being a secondhand piano whose hammers were willfully modified by someone else.

As a way to disguise my disquiet, I broke the silence by talking a blue streak. First, I asked if he knew that Yichang in Hubei, China, was well-known for their piano manufacturing and that they'd developed different techniques in making the instrument. I added that they needed a large number of technicians. I could start from scratch and learn everything. Maybe one day I'd be a technician of international standing.

I didn't make this up on the spot to cover my embarrassment. The possibility had occurred to me six months earlier, but for some reason, I'd had trouble talking about it in front of him.

For him things always took new turns, and he could start over if mistakes were made. So, he never considered the cost and risk others might face with every step they took.

The car stopped at a nineteenth-century estate that appeared to have been in disuse for years. A small wooden plaque on the barbed wire fence simply stated "Pianos for sale." It was hard to imagine that this was the largest secondhand piano wholesaler in the state of New York. Two hundred meters beyond where we were was an enormous warehouse, next to which was what appeared to be a factory, with thick smoke rising from its chimney.

"Let me think about it," I said. "I'll decide before I get on the plane the day after tomorrow."

"There are too many distractions in life, all very bothersome.
"I'm disgusted with myself. That's all."

Richter: The Enigma ends with that comment from the maestro. How disappointing.

Luckily, you'll never get old, so you don't need to know how lonely it will be.

Maybe I'll never become a top piano tuner.

The distance between me and excellence at the moment was that I too am disgusted with myself. That's all.

The owner's son, Daniel, met us at the warehouse entrance. Third generation. A paunchy man, but a smooth talker when it came to business; he started off by telling us about his supply source. Usually, he purchased them at auctions; some he bought from shuttered piano stores and some he got cheaply from creditors of bankrupt factories. Seven to eight hundred pianos came and went through his place each year, with containers of them shipped from all over the world.

"Of course, there are also owners who are in a hurry to get rid of a piano. They're usually from neighboring states and have to find a way to bring the item over." Daniel winked at us and made a face showing how impossible the situation was, yet failing to conceal his delight.

"Sometimes it does amaze me. Children who are eager to clean out their dead parents' house for sale or divorcing couples dividing up their property can't wait to virtually give away a beautiful piano. I once paid two hundred for an ebony upright. Can you believe that? Those were the same pianos that had been moved into their houses amid admiration and happy cheers."

We headed to the warehouse, passing through a metal gate on a passageway strewn with piano parts, metal frames piled high, hammers that had been dug out of broken pianos, and keyboards and soundboards casually pushed up against the wall. Dust rose as we walked by.

I asked Daniel about the chimney in the next building.

"Oh, that." He continued calmly with a wave of his hand, "We do our best to salvage parts from the used pianos to fix others that still look fine on the outside. Parts we can't use right away are put here. These nonflammable ones will eventually be dumped like garbage. After all the usable parts are removed, the cases are burned in a furnace. With such a large space, it would cost too much to heat with electricity or oil. See there, that's the furnace opening. We keep the place warm by burning the wood from pianos so others can have a second chance."

Before me emerged a picture of a piano curling up and blackening in fire.

It was like night and day when you compared this place with the pretty storefronts in Midtown. How many of the secondhand instruments on display there had been sent to a concentration camp like this, a solitary cell in an insane asylum?

The furnace was on the other end of the archway, but I thought I could hear the crackling fire.

Burning discarded pianos alone obviously did not produce enough heat to adequately warm the warehouse, for icy air kept rising up from my feet as I followed Daniel through one door after another.

An arched passageway ended with steps leading down. At the foot of the stairs, I was greeted by a warehouse the size of two basketball courts.

A windowless space. Under several dim lights piano carcasses floated amid an ocean of dust. About a hundred pianos were waiting, some with a dismantled shell, some missing soundboards, some still in filthy bubble wrap, all looking pitiful, fearful, their lives hanging by a thread.

I had thoughts of the unlighted cargo hold of a slave ship, the pleading eyes of those on the verge of death.

Pianos without lids, with broken legs or their insides emptied out. Batches of actions, loops of copper wire hanging on the wall, still twitching like nerves without the protection of flesh and blood. Like a cellar in horror movies, these pianos looked more like hostages a deranged criminal had captured from around the world to do what he pleased with here. Except for a few still in good enough shape to be resold, the pianos would be dismembered or reassembled. Would the reconstructed pianos feel schizophrenic?

Lin and Daniel were off in a corner talking next to a row of carved wooden boards leaning against the wall.

Delicate maple, graceful ebony, sturdy mahogany, steady birch, all lined up, calling to mind fates like a deck of tarot cards waiting to be knocked over.

Facing such an enormous piano cemetery, rather than horror or grief, I felt the joy of a whale that has finally located a deserted island where its dying companions have gathered, wishing it had happened earlier.

I couldn't say when I started hearing calls made by carcasses like these coming from somewhere, but that day had finally come. At last I'd found them, and we were together.

I struggled to find a path as they rushed up to surround me.

Very soon, liberation . . .

In the tenderest tone, I transformed myself into Mother Teresa comforting soldiers wounded in battle and said a prayer for all the disfigured pianos around me.

You spent your lives serving humanity's vanity and vulgarity. I know how hard it was for you.

Over the centuries, so few of you were lucky enough to be blessed by geniuses and the finest musical talents. Most of you lived in vain. Putting myself in your shoes, I realize that my life hasn't been all that different from yours. By the way, I don't think I mentioned that I never got my music degree.

Their reason to expel me was, I sneaked into a music classroom one night and poured sulfuric acid on the four oldest pianos. But I had no recollection of doing any of that.

The Steinway was the only piano I'd damaged.

I could never bring myself to do that if I'd known that a defaced piano would end up in a place like this. I'm no piano executioner. I'm a piano tuner. The job of a tuner is to do his best to cover up your defects and make you charming and delightful, so you'll be treasured and adored. I wouldn't—

It wasn't me! It wasn't me! It wasn't me!

The angry howl came so suddenly I was seeing stars. With blurred vision, I saw Lin and Daniel running toward me.

It was then I noticed a hammer in my hand that I did not remember picking up. Looking down, I saw an old piano with a broken leg lying at my feet, its lid hacked to pieces.

In retrospect, it was truly humiliating to be grabbed and tossed out the door by the workers.

I still couldn't explain how it all happened. Lin *san* told me he paid Daniel five hundred. I do remember apologizing incoherently and repeatedly to him in the parking lot.

"I don't think I can . . . I can't . . . help you now. I'm sorry, I really can't. I mean it . . ."

He was quiet at first, and then he shouted my name:

"Hu—Yi—lu!"

He wrapped his arms around me, for I was shaking hysterically and uncontrollably.

His Taiwanese-accented Mandarin sounded like Japanese at first, like *oishi* or *kawai*. When I finally realized he was calling me, I was momentarily lost. Should I wail or burst out laughing?

As I leaned weakly against his shoulder, I saw that the two of us, dressed in black, stood in an empty lot covered in a night's snowfall like broken black keys.

Black keys are separated from each other by other keys, unlike the white keys that nestle up against one another. Isn't that right?

Then I heard him take out a ring of keys.

"Take care of the piano at my house before my return. Can you do that?"

Looking at his hand, I recalled the pain caused by a promise a very long time ago.

12

In 1999, during one of NHK World's late-night broadcasts, a thirty-minute program of music featured a nearly seventy-year-old pianist whom no one had heard of. Ingrid Fuziko Hemming was born in Berlin in 1932 to a Swedish painter and architect of Russian descent and a Japanese mother, a piano teacher. The family moved back to Japan when she was five, but her father had trouble adjusting to life there and returned to Sweden alone, leaving his wife and two children. In 1961, Fuziko went to study in Germany but had to give up after a cold affected her hearing.

Since then she had drifted for more than three decades before quietly returning to Japan in 1995 to take up piano teaching. The program was not a popular one, but this particular episode caught viewers' eyes. An old woman, with mixed-race parents, eccentrically dressed, was both mysterious and sad.

A few months later, her first album was released, with meteoric record sales of three hundred thousand in just three months.

"I'm sure you don't think much of her playing, typical conservatory style, meeting every requirement but lacking flair, you'd say."

"Let's put that aside. I just want to use this as an example to show you how the times have changed since your absence."

A superb pianist cannot compete with someone with a story to tell. Musicians of your generation would never guess that an aging woman rising against the trends would draw so much more attention than a prodigy.

What would Glenn Gould say?

He believed that recording was the right path and refused to perform in concerts. But he'd forgotten that in his time, no one would notice his records if he hadn't played well in concerts.

The lady thoroughly carried out his idea by completely skipping concert performance and directly becoming a legendary figure. It was all because of a twenty-first-century phenomenon, online promotion, that an overlooked program was posted over and over; otherwise, an old woman playing pieces by Liszt would have been drowned out by other noise.

More than a million and a half copies of her album were sold. After being randomly selected by the God of Fortune and selling so many copies, she spent the next twenty years giving concerts all over the world, as if it were the real proof of her existence.

She was nearing ninety. With residences in Paris, Berlin, Tokyo, and New York, she continued living a solitary life, wearing an indifferent expression, as if she'd gotten used to being a citizen of the world.

She never married, nor was she ever in love, she claimed. How she got through the lonely life of a world traveler only she knew.

If you still had your physical body, Joseph, would you want to get old like this?

Or would you admit wholeheartedly that you could not hope to be so fierce and intrepid?

She might as well have been the concretized image of classical music in the minds of average people. Ancient, doddering, stubborn, mad, inscrutable. There were reasons why so many were fascinated by her.

Maybe we've all missed the black humor hidden in classical music.

One dark night two hundred years ago, an ambitious man losing his hearing decided to write a symphony on fate. Would the thought of doing that make him laugh? Could the whole piece have been written when he was slightly deranged, laughing and baying?

Yet when it was performed on stage, all the musicians were prim and proper, highly focused on controlling every note so nothing would be amiss.

Ironically, fate was the most difficult thing to control at a performance.

It always quietly changes your intended path without your knowing it. Some rise to fame effortlessly while others plunge downward. Which segment caught the attention of the God of Fortune? Hindsight, however clear, does not help matters, like a lost piece in a jigsaw puzzle.

I had the feeling that fate was playing a trick on me while I played the role of narrator.

As a tuner, I knew little about metafiction, deconstruction, and parody; I was just trying to relay everything I recalled. There was nothing I could do if I somehow alarmed fate, and I would have to wait to see how fate reevaluated me.

That was all I knew.

Right, no one would believe that I was being unprofessional by leaving the Steinway to deteriorate in that empty house, would they?

Trust me, it would eventually find a new tuner.

Just like your Steinway. It finally showed up before me, twenty-five years later.

If you have a chance to run into Richter in the other world, please tell him this: I understand the difference between his self-disgust and my self-loathing.

Self is the deficiency that average people can never over-come, while for him it was merely a burden of illusion.

Which one were you?

With my eyes on the sheet music, I played for two hours until I managed to make it through Schubert's 18th Piano Sonata from start to finish. I stopped to pick up a pencil and make a few notations on the sheet before get-ting ready to try again. My fingers, however, had a mind of their own, and on a whim launched into a lighthearted lieder.

> *A boy espied, in the morning light,*
> *a little rosebud blowing.*

As a second-grader, I happily sang along with the class, accompanied by our teacher, our pure, innocent voices lighting up the music classroom. It was this piece I stayed to play after class when the teacher overheard me playing the chords without being taught.

How could an unknown man, who was short and afflicted with syphilis, write a piece so bright, as if bedewed? A breeze of passing time stirred up ripples. I closed my eyes and calmed my mind before my hands found the spot on the keyboard in the dark and struck the first note in the sonata.

What happened next would be an encore piece to the story—

Even though I knew that you would be the only one generous enough to give me a standing ovation.

On the sixteenth floor of a building in the middle of Moscow.

I did not fly back to Taipei after leaving New York; nor did I land in Yichang, Hubei. Instead, I decided to visit Richter's old house.

It was in the afternoon, a light snow falling. I'd thought I could see the small apartment the two of them first moved into, but this was the only place open to visitors. He'd moved here with Nina in 1971 in new government housing for artists.

Never formally married, they were assigned two units, which were then turned into one, with two entrances.

After paying five hundred rubles, I waited for the grannie guard to get hold of an English-speaking guide, who showed me into the unit on the left. If I hadn't been told beforehand, I wouldn't have known who could have lived behind the door.

The unit had virtually no trace of Nina's life, except for her portrait hanging in the study where she also taught, and a peeling Becker.

All the furniture in the bedroom had been cleared out. The walls were filled with Richter's paintings, giving music fans a chance to appreciate his other talents. The dining room was repurposed to display items from his childhood, along with his mother's diary with the entry:

"I knew the child was a prodigy!"

I walked up to study a crayon drawing that featured bright colors and lively strokes; it was a publicity poster that the child maestro created for a musical he wrote.

Contrary to the sense of their daily life I'd hope to get, everything in the room was artificially arranged for display. The guide told me that Nina had spent years working hard to collect and list these items.

Leaving the dining room, we came to the space where the dividing wall had been. The living rooms in both units combined with the dining room on his side to form a bright, spacious music room, where he had given small concerts. The unequal distribution of space seemed to have existed when they were both alive. It had always been like that. Nina gave singing lessons in her small study, while Richter had his own, large music room.

His side no longer had a dining room, so does that mean he went to her side to eat?

Did they often eat together at home?

When she was cooking, did she miss the old Richter, when he had yet to have his own space? Was she happy with their union?

No guide could answer these kinds of idiosyncratic questions.

His music room was big enough to accommodate two grand Steinways. The guide proudly led me to one of them, telling me that the maestro practiced on it. I wanted to ask him if he knew that Richter only played a Yamaha in later concerts.

Richter spent most of his time overseas in his later years, so he probably did not come back here often. But the two pianos had to keep playing their roles to produce an illusion for tourists. *There they are! The one-of-a-kind pianos the maestro used to hone his extraordinary skill!* I was reminded of workers at amusement parks, dressed up like cartoon characters to draw in customers. I felt sorry for the two Steinways.

More like forgotten, they weren't being preserved here. It was sad enough that no one would be playing them; worse yet, they were dressed up to present a happy scene for pilgrims to be photographed alongside.

At least they had each other. When the doors were locked at night, they could reminisce about the past together. But they might never know that the maestro was actually imagining the pianissimo on another piano when he played one of them.

I didn't know Russian, so I had no idea whose books lined Richter's shelves. Finally, I came to Richter's bedroom after meandering as if in a labyrinth.

It was a cramped space, large enough for only a single bed.

I stared silently at a bed that was far less roomy and comfortable than a sofa in anyone else's house. Did he die on this bed? I finally asked the guide.

"Oh, no. He died in a hospital, after a heart attack, while working on a concert performance. The last piece he played was Schubert's piano sonata no. 3. He said his favorite was No. 18, D. 894—"

"Was he practicing here?" I had to cut him off.

He was taken aback.

"No, in his dacha in the western suburb."

Before leaving, I asked the guide if I could play a few notes on one of the Steinways. Just a few. He actually agreed. I knew he was trying to cater to a tourist, but I couldn't help feeling elated.

Yet, when I returned to the music room and stared at the two pianos standing there quietly together, my out-stretched right index finger hesitated.

Wouldn't it be cruel to stir and awaken them, believing they would be on stage again?

Why not let them remain in their slumber? I turned around and walked into the blanketing snow that brought me there.

Acknowledgments

This is my first fictional work published in English. What an amazing journey!

I'd like to thank those who have made this memorable journey together with me. Thanks to Howard Goldblatt and Li-chun Lin, for their meticulous and beautiful translation. Thanks to my editor, Cal Barksdale, at Arcade for his support and belief in the book. Whitney Hsu, my agent at Andrew Nurnberg Associates in Taiwan, has been such an enthusiastic advocate and deserves a round of loud applause. To Vivian Chen, my publisher in Taiwan, without your keen literary sense and professionalism, *The Piano Tuner* couldn't have started its first step and received such wide attention afterward.

Last but not the least, my love to Rahmaninov and Sviatoslav Richter, who are the inspiration for this novel and became my guardian angels along the way.